THE FRENCH FATHER

ALAIN ELKANN

THE FRENCH FATHER

Translated from the Italian
by Alastair McEwen

Pushkin Press
London

English translation © Alastair McEwen 2011

First published in Italian as
Il padre francese © Romanzo Bompiani 1999

This edition first published in 2011 by
Pushkin Press
12 Chester Terrace
London NW1 4ND

British Library Cataloguing in Publication Data:
A catalogue record for this book is available
from the British Library

ISBN 978 1 906548 34 6

All rights reserved. No part of this publication may be
reproduced, stored in a retrieval system or transmitted in
any form or by any means, electronic, mechanical,
photocopying, recording or otherwise,
without prior permission in writing from
Pushkin Press

Cover: *Paris Street Rainy Day* 1877 Gustave Caillebotte
© Charles H and Mary F S Worcester Collection
The Art Institute of Chicago

Frontispiece: Alain Elkann
© Jean-Philippe Baltes/SIPA PRESS

Set in 11 on 15 Baskerville Monotype
and printed on Munken Print 80 gsm
by MPG Books Group

www.pushkinpress.com

For my sister Brigitte

You are always your parents' son,
even after their death
                Anonymous

To save a man is to save the whole
world
                Talmud

THE FRENCH FATHER

M Y SISTER'S NAME IS YVONNE. She is a good-looking forty-four, petite, with light chestnut hair cut short, a small, slightly arched nose, full lips and very expressive blue eyes. An impulsive, authoritarian character, she always says what she thinks. She is understanding with the people she loves. Yvonne has always been present in the important moments of my life and, apart from a few normal, short-lived quarrels, we have always got along.

When our father died, neither of us could believe it. The handsome hero, strict, cruel, very much loved and feared by both of us, the man who had cemented our bond, had gone for ever. In silence, we accompanied him to the cemetery together, sitting close to each other in the hearse as it drove through the streets of Paris.

There were a lot of people at Montparnasse cemetery on that cold November morning, and I almost felt as though I was trespassing on a film set. I couldn't concentrate on anything and listened absently to the Rabbi, who was delivering his funeral speech in solemn and moving tones, recalling my father's merits and commemorating his works and deeds. I looked at the light-coloured wooden coffin a few steps away, and refused to believe that it contained his body, not long dead. A few minutes later that coffin would be lowered for ever into the family tomb where my grandparents were buried.

I wasn't sad, nor did I cry in the days following the funeral, but I did feel lonely—he was no longer there, I would never see him again, never phone him again, never again hear the low, stern sound of his voice. During the first week of mourning, the Kaddish had to be recited every evening, and a rabbi and ten Jewish men had to be present at the service. My father's wife was silent, shaken by the enormous void that yawned before her, by the thought of her future solitude.

I went to see her at about eleven the next morning. She greeted me kindly and with embarrassment and, as if we were entering a sanctuary, she took me to my father's dressing room where she opened his closets saying, "Take any suits you want," or, "Take his shirts, pyjamas, socks."

The idea of owning and wearing my father's clothes made me feel vaguely uneasy. As a child, I had always regarded those extremely orderly closets with reverence: his shiny black shoes, all the same, his dark ties, his white handkerchiefs … After his death, these unattainable things had become mine. I could wear the blue pin-striped suit he wore on the day the President of the Republic had awarded him the Legion of Honour, or the morning suit he had worn at my sister's wedding.

Eleven months after our father died, as required by Jewish tradition, Yvonne and I went to the cemetery together for the first anniversary of his death. In the car we didn't talk much, this first visit was intimidating. Luckily, it was a pleasant autumn day and, had it not been for the tombs and chapels, I might have thought we were in a public park.

We stood in front of the grey marble tombstone on which his name had been engraved in gold letters. I opened my prayer book and my sister and I recited the Kaddish. We then stood for a couple of minutes in silence, placed two stones on the tomb and moved off.

After a step or two, I saw a new grave, on which a white stone bore the name 'Roland Topor' in black letters. I knew that Topor had been an artist, a writer. I had met him with my ex-wife and recalled having seen the reports of his death in the newspapers. I remembered him with a glass of red wine in his hand, laughing in a rather coarse way and smoking a cigar. It had been one night in Paris, at the house of a painter friend. Aimlessly, my sister and I began to stroll along the paths of the cemetery. She told me she wasn't unhappy. Standing in front of his tomb had not upset her. I felt that our father's death had united us—we were happy together, alone, walking among the graves.

From that day on, I stopped wearing mourning, I no longer wore a black tie, and I started thinking about my father in a different way. He had been a serious man, but one full of fixations and taboos, a stubborn Capricorn, a moralist with some immoral traits; he laughed little and talked a lot, but when he did laugh, he had a nice smile. My relationship with him was never easy, because one word too many meant being judged severely and incurred some kind of punishment. The most irritating thing about his character, which sometimes harmed him, was his excessiveness, which on occasion verged on extremes of cruelty, precision, strictness, exactitude. The excessive orderliness of his life and his person. Everything was studied, organised, prepared well in advance; nothing was left to chance. Even his clothing was thought out in minute detail—which shirt, which cufflinks, whether a dark suit or a light one, blue or grey. My father also had a very curious relationship with food. He had been on a diet for years and years; he wanted to be slim at all costs, because he found that attractive. He had a horror of paunches and bald heads. He abhorred sweet foods, drank only Evian water and no alcohol. During the night, he used to eat fruit: apples, oranges, tangerines, strawberries and cherries.

He slept badly, took too many sleeping pills and woke very early. Breakfast was of enormous importance. Decaffeinated coffee, ordinary coffee, tea, tea with milk, orange juice, cereals and cooked fruit. It depended on how he was feeling. I had seen him eat quantities of oysters, before he eliminated crustaceans and seafood from his diet. Then there was the period when he ate Emmenthal cheese instead of fruit, then came the period of chicory, endive or lettuce heart salads, seasoned with lots of vinegar and seed oil. When he was young—up to forty-five—he liked steak and large hamburgers. This was followed by long years of grilled fish and nothing else, but when he fell ill, he stopped eating that. For a lifetime he had a real passion for pasta, which he preferred English-style, with butter and Gruyère, or butter and Parmesan. But he knew that starch is fattening, so there was an irreconcilable conflict between his desire for pasta and his rigorous diet.

During his illness, when he found he could eat anything he wanted without putting on weight, he rediscovered his taste for sweets, especially semolina, tapioca, rice, cheesecake, and chocolate ice cream. He started going to an Italian restaurant near his office almost every day. He found it ideal, because it was simple, cheap, and the restaurant owner was from Modena.

My father had always been on ambivalent terms with Italians. On the one hand, he despised their bourgeoisie, especially industrialists, whom he considered insincere, unreliable toadies, whereas he liked waiters, workers and craftsmen. He made friends with a certain Luciano, who was an interior decorator and had decorated various offices for him. He had blind faith in Luciano's taste and, more than anything, he liked talking with him. I never knew what they talked about. Besides a few childhood friends, my father had no friends. He had no love for social life, and didn't play cards. In the evening, he used to read or watch the television. He was reluctant to use the telephone. I was always afraid to make calls in his presence, because he would lose patience. His preference was to communicate by letter or by fax. His papers were always in order, and he was meticulous and precise. He would often use a pencil to tot up his accounts; otherwise he would use a small Japanese calculator. Weight was an obsession for him, which was why he always travelled with his own white scales, since he didn't trust those he found occasionally in hotels. In addition, he took the greatest care with his image, so that no one could ever doubt that he was intelligent, handsome, rich and, above all, a manager. He also needed long moments of solitude, which he devoted to reading history and biographies, but mostly financial papers and dailies. Even when he was very ill, he carried on reading the newspapers day after day. He was a charmer, proud of being attractive to beautiful women and—naturally—of not giving himself to them. Knowing that he was seductive was enough for him. Excess in anything was abhorrent to him and consequently he would never betray any sign of emotional upheaval or suffering. He wanted to appear a cold, hard, severe man, with icy eyes. He wanted to be loved but, above all, feared, and looked upon with respect and admiration. His wish was to be considered a special person, unique, above the others. Even as a Jew, he wanted to be superior, a king consulting with his rabbis.

Since my father died, I have often spoken with his wife, who cannot accept the pain of his loss.

I went to see her one Sunday and found her wandering through the rooms of her flat, as if looking for her husband. Every so often, she would stop and ask me, "What will become of me? Where shall I end up? I can't go on like this, I want to die." Poor woman, she was really desperate.

She and my father had been passionately in love for years. I remember them as if they were two Hollywood stars. She, blonde and very elegant, looked like Grace Kelly; he, dark with green eyes and a white dinner jacket, looked like Cary Grant. When we were on holiday, they would go out in the evenings and, from the balcony of my hotel room, I used to watch them get into a large sports car. To me, they seemed extraordinary, unattainable.

She was an attentive wife, a slave to her husband's every whim or desire, but he feared her sulks, her long silences ...

As a child, I used to go to Paris for my holidays and was surprised by the fact that my father sat at the head of the table and was the only one to talk. He would give an account of his working day, his appointments, what so-and-so had said, and what he had said in reply. He had an extraordinary ability to turn everything to his advantage, so that he would look like a hero to his family. His wife lived vicariously through these accounts of his doings. She led a very private life, looking after the house and the grandchildren.

I didn't know much about my father. He kept his secrets to himself. I always thought of him as an immanent presence, a sort of god sitting in judgement who was always right while I was always wrong. But I also sensed that his disapproval was a way of letting me feel his love, that love typical of northern Jews, rather severe and reserved.

After the visit to the cemetery with my sister, something changed in my relationship with my father. It was as though he had been resurrected within me and I had suddenly seen a new side of his life—not another prestigious position, nor another trip, but his death. Yes, his death, which for me became a new life—the man I had had to share with so many others was now all mine. And now that he was dead, he was no longer the strict person I had lived with for forty-five years, but had become cheerful. As a boy, I found any comparison with him humiliating. I was well aware that he was a handsome man, respected, elegant and honest, who had nothing to fear from anyone, least of all from his son. On many occasions, I had thought that I would have been the first to die. Relations between us were tense, because the threat of punishment always loomed. To disagree with him was dangerous. No confession could be made to him because it might irritate him, and when he judged something to be bad, he never forgot it, and was capable of bringing it up even years later.

On reflecting on Montparnasse cemetery, however, and Roland Topor's neighbouring tomb, I had to smile.

Topor had died young. He had led a dissolute life, one completely devoted to excess: tobacco, alcohol, food, women, disorderly work, sleepless nights. He had been an illustrator, a painter, and a writer whose works had a touch of the macabre about them. I recall his large, dark, darting, slightly bulging eyes, his droll gaze, his rejection of melancholy and self-pity. To tell the truth, I don't know much about Roland Topor, except that he was the opposite of my father and that, when they were alive, they would never have been friends. My father, however, delighted in conversation; he liked to talk about himself and his life. It may be that when they buried Topor a few months after him, he was curious to know about this new person who was to rest beside him for ever. My father was a serious-minded, solemn man, but at times he would laugh heartily. I don't know when it happened, nor how long afterwards, but I am certain that Roland too, on realising there was company in the neighbouring tomb and not used to being alone, spoke to my father in a cheerful and open manner, with the pretext of asking for information about the cemetery. Having been there now for some months and probably bored by being alone with his parents, my father would have replied willingly to Roland's questions. He may have assumed his habitual solemn and serious attitude, that of one who is familiar with the rules and teaches them to others. Roland, who had only just arrived and was unaware of how things stood, must have felt the need to speak to that older man resting in the next tomb, who could give him useful information about living there. After the customary small talk, Roland might have said, "Have you been dead long?"

"No, since the end of November last year. I died of cancer. What did you die of?"

"I died of a stroke."

"So you didn't suffer. How old are you?"

"Fifty-six."

"But that's very young! I died when I was nearly seventy-five, after a long and painful illness. Why did you die so young?"

"Perhaps I didn't think my life was very important. So I ruined it, I overdid things. But then, how can we know? Unfortunately I was a hypochondriac and afraid of doctors and should have had a check-up. But now it's too late—that's the way it went."

"What was your job?"

"Painter, writer, artist."

"Ah, like my son! They're risky professions. You have to be successful!"

"That's right, and what did you do?"

"I've always been in business, in industry and then in banking. But you see, I was a Jew and for many years I looked after the Jewish community."

"I was a Jew too, of Polish origin."

"Where were you born?"

"In Paris."

"Ah, you too! My parents—they're resting here with me now—were from Alsace. Jewish communities have changed a lot. If you're of Polish origin, you must know something about that! Nowadays religious Jews come mostly from North Africa: Algerians, Moroccans, Tunisians, Egyptians."

"Were you religious?"

"Yes, in my own way very much so, but not Orthodox. I was President of the Community."

"I think I must have heard about you from one of my aunts, who was my one remaining connection with religion. I'm telling you this because I remember that she always used to say, 'You should see our President, he's as handsome as a film star.' Were you a handsome man? Did you look like an American actor?"

"Well, in short, I don't know; it's not for me to say. As a matter of fact I think I was handsome, and always tried to look respectable, elegant. But I must confess that it still upsets me, despite the fact that I've been dead for more than a year, to talk about the Jewish community. This is nothing new, but Jews are stupid, ungrateful, and solidarity is not their strong point. Unfortunately, that's the truth. Just imagine, in my place they elected a vulgar person without culture, only because he let it be understood that he had a lot of money and had promised favours left and right. I had chosen as my successor an upright and worthy man, the President of the Constitutional Court. There was nothing doing, however. I had underestimated money's power to corrupt, and so they elected him instead of the magistrate I had designated. I considered it an insult and so I withdrew from the community. It was a great sorrow to realise that so many years of work had been wiped out in an instant. The community was the chief interest in my life. I am well aware that in the elections I was betrayed by the Grand Rabbi of France. There's no such thing as gratitude, that's a fact. I was the one who got him to come from Marseilles. I had to oblige the community to accept him, not without difficulty, and he, as a token of his gratitude, allowed himself to be seduced by the new candidate who took him up in his private plane and provided him with certain comforts ... The only friends I have left are two old rabbis, an Algerian—highly intelligent and a philosopher— and another from Alsace, more of a diplomatic type, less intellectual. I used to see them on Sunday mornings, we would talk together and they taught me about Jewish philosophy, which I have always been enthusiastic about. For all my life I have always been very proud to be a Jew. I should think that you too, even though you chose art, are proud to be a Jew. I was well acquainted with Arthur Rubinstein, the pianist. We used to have Seder, the Passover dinner, together. They were strange years, the ones before I died. I was terrified that I had prostate trouble, then there was the trauma over my pension, which I absolutely did not want to accept. I solved the problem by setting up a little bank that bears my name. Thank God my family life has never been a burden. I must say that I like my second wife very much: blonde, not very tall, well-proportioned, long slender legs, blue eyes, a little nose like a baby's, and very soft, smooth skin. She was a quiet woman and never asked questions; she never disturbed me when I was working, and left me free during the day. We always spent the evenings together. My mother didn't like her at all, but then she hated all the women who had anything to do with me. My father was indifferent, he never showed his feelings. It's strange, for years I mourned my parents, I used to talk about them to my children, and I would go to the synagogue on the anniversary of their deaths, yet now that we've been back together for over a year, I feel that they're less close, absent. It's as though I were disturbing them. You see, they died within a few months of each other, and they've been here for over thirty years. I used to come to visit them once a year. I believe that after a while dead people's memories fade away. Then there's the language problem. Now they're dead, they speak only Alsatian dialect, their real tongue, which I have never spoken. I never wanted to speak dialects, or Yiddish. As a boy, I wanted to be French, a Parisian. I was somewhat ashamed, I must confess, of having a mother with a foreign accent, German. What's more, Yiddish seemed to be a language that segregates Jews, puts them in a ghetto, and I wanted nothing to do with it!"

"Pardon me for interrupting, but how could you have been the President of a Jewish community for so many years if you can't speak Yiddish? I can't believe it. I come from a family of non-religious Jews, people who worked in the theatre, yet they all spoke Yiddish, and even I can get out a few words."

"Yes, I know, but speaking Yiddish is not very important in France nowadays. Most French Jews come from North Africa and can speak Arabic, but not Yiddish. And then, you must understand, I was born in Paris, in the ninth *arrondissement*, and only when I was six did my parents move to the sixteenth, an upper-middle-class area, where the rich Jews lived, who then—before the war—were from Alsace. My father fought in the trenches during the first war and was awarded the Military Cross. He wanted to feel that he was French, a patriot. I studied for admission to the Polytechnic, to become an engineer, to belong to an elite. I wanted to become an important person. We were French citizens of the Jewish faith, not particularly religious, well-off. In June 1940, I recall that we were lunching with my parents, an aunt and her husband, at the restaurant in the Hôtel Raphaël, an elegant place a stone's throw from the Étoile, when the *maître* came up in a very agitated manner and said to my father, "Mr Elkann, the Germans are at Versailles." My father had underestimated Hitler and believed that we French would easily have won the war, but since he was a determined and calm man, as soon as he learnt the news, he asked for the bill, paid it, and when we were in the car he said to the driver, without wasting words, "We're going to Vichy." We owned a holiday home there, where my mother's mother had gone to live. So we left Paris, my life, my friends, and my destiny changed. My parents sent me to New York, where my uncle from Basle was living. He had been working there for years and had become a millionaire. The trip wasn't easy. I left by train for Marseilles, but couldn't get a ship. I found a flight for Casablanca, where they put me in prison, since I didn't have the necessary visa. When I managed to have myself released, I took another plane to Lisbon, where a ship was leaving for

New York. But my papers were not in order, so I ended up in prison again. When they released me, I finally embarked for New York, where they put me in prison on Staten Island. I was eighteen and felt I was having a great adventure. Alone in the world, fleeing from one country to another, from one prison to another, I found myself in America and it all seemed an incredible exploit.

"My uncle, who became my guardian, was an outstanding person. After studying at the Zurich Polytechnic, he emigrated to the United States where he set up a chemical-products firm and married an American actress. He and his wife lived in a hotel and, although he had become American, he continued to eat only German-Swiss food, which a cook from Basle prepared for him. His greatest delight was playing practical jokes, such as putting a rubber mouse on a lady's thigh, for example. Being very rich gave him the assured air of someone who can do more or less what he wants. He liked to have well-ironed hundred-dollar bills in his pocket and would give them to anyone he met, according to his whim. Once, I asked him, 'Why do you give money even to people who don't need it?'

"'Because it's always a pleasure!'

"My uncle had little to do with me, and delegated his guardianship to a very serious and well-mannered gentleman, who worked for him.

"I enrolled in the faculty of engineering, where I met other Jewish refugees in New York, as well as Americans. At that time, I was fat and gluttonous. I had no money and ate only bread and mayonnaise in coffee shops. On Sundays, I used to go with a friend to the Waldorf Astoria, where there were grand receptions for weddings, silver weddings, christenings and first communions. We pretended to be guests and so we could eat and drink as much as we wanted. Once I got drunk and fell down while I was dancing. Since then, I have almost never drunk anything, but we Jews are not drinkers!"

"That's what you say! I died from a cerebral ischemia, because I have always drunk, eaten and smoked too much. I had had a few warning signs, but for me there would have been no point in carrying on living if I had had to be careful about everything, prudent, no drinking, no smoking. I was making love up to a few minutes before I died. I have loved many women and in some cases I have made them suffer, but believe me, I am neither a cynic nor cruel. Life's like that and if it weren't for wine, I don't even know how you could bear it! My people were Poles, non-drinkers, but I was born in Paris … "

"I have always attached great importance to the fact of being a Jew, but my relationship with France changed after the war. The French had been fascists, they had collaborated with the Nazis, they had betrayed the Jews and let them be exterminated in the death camps. You must know this, even if you were only a child! After the war, I decided to go back and live in Paris, but I often yearned for America. My son, on the other hand, was educated in Italy. He speaks Italian, and has almost always lived in Italy."

"Lucky him! I have had a lot of exhibitions there. I have a great many Italian friends, but I don't speak the language. Do you speak Italian?"

"No, and not even German. My first wife was Italian, we met in New York during the war. I was fond of her, she was very devoted. But I wasn't happy with her, and that's how I met the woman who would become my second wife. With her, I liked staying in bed, making love. We had a daughter, but I was never much of a family man, I've always preferred work, the office, deciding, asserting my point of view, being esteemed for my intelligence. Certainly, I've never been sorry to know that I was a handsome man, I must say. Especially when I lost weight, I felt more handsome, more elegant. Then, when my parents died, I started taking an interest in religion, taking part in community life. Dealing with Jews and Jewish matters. I have always been a worker, because if you want to live well, in luxury, you need a lot of money, and, unfortunately, my uncle in America didn't leave me anything. I thought I would have been his natural heir, but he preferred to leave everything he had to the Zoological Gardens in Basle and to a foundation. That's how I didn't become a millionaire. I apologise for boring you with this story. I know I talk a lot, but I haven't spoken with anyone for months and months, so I had to get things off my chest! How long is it since you arrived?"

"About a month, not more."

"How do you like it?"

"I don't know yet. Death caught me unprepared. I don't remember much. I'm not used to living alone, not smoking, not drinking, not laughing, not talking, not drawing, and not expressing myself. When you die suddenly, still young, it's true you're out of the way, but there are a few problems. In short, you're no longer alive and you're no longer a nuisance to anyone, but you're not there. I should have liked to settle my debts with the Inland Revenue, before dying. It would have been better for my poor son!"

"And your parents?"

"They're buried somewhere else. They lived in another district. I shan't see them again."

"Do you miss life?"

"I don't know. I was tired out when I died, and I didn't know it. I never rested. I worked, went out, drank, ate, never slept. I never had enough time. Now there's all the time in the world."

Since I had taken an interest in Roland Topor as the occupant of the tomb next to my father's, besides reading his books and getting to know his works, I felt that I wanted to talk about him to someone who had been close to him.

Stefania, an Italian friend who had lived in Paris for years, suggested that I talk to Nicolas, Roland's only son by his first wife. After a complicated search, I managed to contact him.

"Are you Nicolas, Roland Topor's son?"

"Yes, I am." It was the voice of a young, shy person.

"I'm the son of the man who is buried next to your father, and I've called because I should like to talk about our fathers. I hope I'm not disturbing you."

"No, I don't feel like talking about my father. It's not something I can do yet."

"I should like to go to the cemetery with you. Your father's grave is very spartan. My father is buried beside his parents. How is it that your grandparents aren't buried beside your father?"

"Just a minute, who are you? I don't even know you. I've told you that I don't want to talk about this matter, you ask me why my grandparents aren't buried together with my father, and you expect an answer? And, what's more, I must tell you that the stone you saw on my father's grave is a temporary one. But this is none of your business and, as I told you, I don't want to talk about it."

"Do you mean you'll move him? You'll bury him somewhere else, with his parents?"

"Not at all. I have nothing to say about this, I don't want to talk. Call me some other time. Today is a holiday."

"What do you do for a living?"

"I'm sorry, I have nothing further to say, I don't feel like it."

Clearly, our relations had got off on the wrong foot. I shouldn't have phoned him, or I should have been more tactful, less direct. I should have persuaded him to meet me, but not at the cemetery. One fact remained uncertain—I hadn't understood if Nicolas was really upset by his father's sudden death. Perhaps they were on bad terms and he hadn't managed to set things right before his father died. Perhaps Roland had left debts and there wasn't enough money for a nice tomb. Perhaps it wasn't the son who had dealt with the burial.

By chance, on the very evening that I had spoken with Nicolas, at the Brasserie Lipp I met Bob, an art dealer who knew Roland well and owned some of his works.

"Of course, Roland was an extraordinary man, his laugh was unforgettable, he used to talk for hours and hours with his friends. In the past few years, he almost always spent his time with a Scandinavian sculptor, Erik. They used to go round the *bistrots* ... I'd advise you to look for Erik, you'll see, he'll be able to tell you a lot. Call me tomorrow, I'll give you his phone number," said Bob.

Next morning, my daughter joined me in a café. She was wearing soft black silk slacks, green gym shoes and a green cotton twinset. Beautiful, still sleepy, she sat down in front of me. She had the fresh, firm skin of an eighteen-year-old, and full lips. Ginevra's look did not immediately reveal her state of mind, because she is a girl whose moods change very easily. She drank an orange juice and ate a croissant. I took a coffee and a croissant. At about ten o'clock, we went to Montparnasse cemetery. She had already been there by herself a few weeks earlier to visit her grandfather's grave. We went in and started looking for our family tomb. First we came to Topor's and took a photo of it, then a few steps further on we photographed my father's. I recited the Kaddish in front of her, and then we went to look for some stones and each of us placed two on the grave. We weren't sad or upset. She wanted to know what other famous people were buried there. On a map we saw the tombs of Sartre, Brâncuşi, Beckett and Baudelaire.

"Baudelaire is very near grandfather! Sartre and de Beauvoir are just over there."

We went to look for Beckett's tomb, which was a very simple slab of grey marble. Looking at tombs is not very moving. It's a little like looking at book covers—they contain the authors of the books.

"How are you feeling? Do you like this cemetery?"

"Yes, but it's a sad, grey day."

Several times that morning Ginevra told me she was sleepy, tired, and the weather was grey. She wasn't sure whether she should go to Naples with her grandparents or not. In the meantime, she would stay in Paris while I had to leave. But I shall be coming back soon, I have to talk to Topor's friends. It's a curious way of continuing to live with my father, whom I miss.

My father's wife is not well. She wants affection, wants to get better. My sister tells her that she absolutely must make an effort, but she can't manage it. She would like someone—anyone—to make that effort gently for her and then not rub it in or, better still, not even let her know they had done it. Now she's back at home, after the hospital. While she was there, I phoned her every day and asked, "How are you feeling?"

"Bad, always the same. I want to end it all, I can't go on any longer, I don't want anything, I'm bored."

When she talked like that, I felt impotent, swinging between grief and anger. Between the desire to say "That's enough now" and the need, on the other hand, to say "Poor thing, I'm sorry". Her future was in the hands of her psychiatrist—he changed her medicines, prescribed the dosages, hospitalised her, looked after her, told her she was better. He always talked like the owner of a hotel in the mountains, who boasts to his guests of its qualities as a ski resort, while allowing a few winks and nods, a hint of malice, to slip into the conversation.

When I went to visit her, she was dressed but dishevelled. We sat in the drawing room, and she said dejectedly, "I really feel ill, I'm very hurt, because your father went before I did. I want to die. If I had a gun, I'd shoot myself … "

She didn't know if she had an appointment with the doctor that afternoon. We tried to reach him on the phone, but he wasn't in. The Portuguese maid came and announced that lunch was served. We ate and spoke little. I tried to buck her up, but all efforts were useless. She dragged herself incessantly from one room to another in her huge apartment. I thought how different it had all been when my father was alive. At lunch, he sat at the head of the table, where she now sat. He used to dine in a dressing gown worn over his pyjamas, with Swedish clogs on his feet. He couldn't bear being dressed indoors. During dinner, he would watch the news and they spoke little to each other.

After lunch, we moved to the library for coffee. We called the doctor again and his secretary said that we had an appointment. When we got into the car, she asked me in a worried tone, "Will you wait for me?"

"Of course."

The doctor, whom I saw for the second time, seemed elusive, ambiguous, but sure of himself in prescribing, changing, modifying and discarding medications. Only two days before, my father's wife had left the hospital where he had put her, and now he prescribed a stay at a psychiatric clinic where they would look after her, just as they were doing with another disconsolate widow, who was also quite old. My father's wife was intimidated, scared and submissive in front of that bald man who was busy writing her prescription. She asked him, "Doctor, shall I get better? Are you sure that it's best to hospitalise me?"

"Yes, absolutely sure."

"When must I go?"

"As soon as possible, this afternoon. I've called them and they're expecting you. They have a room ready for you."

"Will you come to visit me?"

"Yes, once a week. It's very easy to get there. The map on the brochure is very accurate."

We left the doctor's, reassured and astonished at how fast things were moving. We returned home without speaking. It was a summer's day, but the sky was overcast. As soon as we reached the flat, she rushed to pack a couple of suitcases and, accompanied by the Portuguese maid, we left immediately for the clinic. In the car, not a word was said.

She found the clinic distressing, horrible. Her room was spacious with large windows overlooking the park. Once in bed she was desperate, continually saying that she wanted to kill herself, that her husband would never have let her go to a place like that. I asked her, "Would you like to go home? I'll take you."

"No, the doctor said that I must stay here, but I don't want to stay the whole summer, it's not possible."

When I left the clinic I had a terrible headache, I felt useless, incapable, I didn't know what I should do. To see a person losing control and suffering like that is a heavy burden, one that comes with a feeling of total impotence.

In the meantime I was in Paris, so I telephoned Topor's friend, Erik, the sculptor, with whom he got drunk and had fun in the evenings. I told him that Nicolas had taken my phone call badly.

"He must have been upset."

"Yes. I only wanted to tell him that our fathers were buried near each other."

"Of course, but that's just what irritated him, his father's burial. Like me, he wanted Roland to be buried next to his parents in another cemetery, but his sister and his girlfriend were set on Montparnasse. They said that Roland was a great artist, a public figure, and should therefore lie beside other great artists and writers."

"I see, even when you're dead, there are good and bad addresses."

"Nicolas wanted his father to rest beside his grandparents."

"I'll call him back to say I didn't want to offend him. When can we meet?"

"Unfortunately I'm leaving. I have an exhibition to organise in Italy, but we'll get in touch when I come back. OK?"

"Where in Italy?"

"Near Milan. They're very large sculptures. The truck should be here any minute to fetch them, they're bronze."

"When are you leaving?"

"Tomorrow."

"So couldn't we meet just for a moment this evening?"

"No, it won't be possible. I've got too much to do. I can't come into town. We'll meet when I return. Give me a call."

That evening I phoned Topor's son again.

"I really must apologise, I didn't mean to be so inopportune. I felt drawn to you because our fathers are buried next to each other, but I didn't know you were against his being buried there."

"Who told you I was against it?"

"Erik, one of your father's friends."

"Ah, but that's not exactly how it is. The fact is that the place where my father is buried has little to do with it. I defend his work. That's what counts most for me and for him, do you see?"

"You're a painter, aren't you?"

"Yes."

"Was your father happy about your choice of profession?"

"Yes, he had always liked the idea and he encouraged me. He was very critical, inflexible. He wanted me to be strict with myself. Of course, I was well aware that it isn't easy to be a painter nowadays."

"In what way?"

"Well, the French market isn't up to much. I sell most of my work in Belgium."

"I should like to see your work."

"Yes, perhaps you can one day. Now, however, I've got a lot to do, both for my own work and for my father's."

Topor's son had a very sweet voice, like a little boy's. His father, too, had been a very kind man. Perhaps their likeness lay in their kindly manner.

While I was in Paris I had to meet Roman Polanski, the Polish film director whose film *The Tenant* was inspired by one of Topor's books. In both Topor and Polanski there is a desire to exorcise the horrors of the terrible war that both had lived through as persecuted Jewish children.

My father and Roland, too, would have ended up talking about the war. My father might have said, "You see, you were still a child, but I had suffered a terrible humiliation. In New York, as a refugee, I should have liked to enlist with the Free French troops in London, and join General de Gaulle. But at the medical they declared me unfit for military service, because I was afraid of birds. Now I'm dead, I find that all my phobias have disappeared together with my life. Little birds sometimes perch on my tombstone and I don't even notice, in fact I must say that their chirping cheers me up, as does the slight whirr of their beating wings. So, thanks to my ornithophobia, I stayed on in America and worked in an armaments factory. It was a real punishment not to be in London among the men who were preparing the Normandy landings. Perhaps the distaste I felt for General de Gaulle when he returned to power after the Algerian War was connected with the fact that I wasn't able to fight at his side, to be on his general staff. No, I had no merit in the General's eyes since, owing to a stupid phobia, I had not played a part in destiny's great plan to liberate my homeland from the Nazi yoke. Where were you during the war?"

"I escaped with my parents and my sister. We fled because we were Jews and because my father had friends in the Resistance. I remember that the German soldiers used to frighten me, although I liked them. Impeccable in their uniforms, they conveyed something solemn, something menacing, but also pathetic. It was during that time that the desire grew in me to fool around, to change my life, to overcome my fear through laughter, bragging, heavy drinking sessions. Drink makes the timid bold."

"I didn't drink because I didn't want to get fat, and drink puts the pounds on. I didn't want a beer belly. I wanted to be slim, a handsome old man with white hair."

"No, not me! I had fun, I didn't deny myself anything up to my death."

"But perhaps you weren't handsome?"

"No, I was almost bald, and overweight."

"There were two periods in my life. As a boy, I knew I had a handsome face, big green eyes and a small nose, but I was a bit chubby. No belly, but chubby legs, and a bit of a double chin. I was about fifty when I decided to diet, become very thin and elegant. That way, I could wear close-fitting suits and not have to wear baggy clothes to hide the fact that I was overweight. Afterwards it was a continual exercise of will, trying not to get fat again and to stay thin. But I must be repeating myself, because I already told you about my physical appearance."

"It doesn't matter. You're sincere, you're not ashamed of being vain. And your children?"

"I haven't seen much of my children. I don't know what I would have wanted from them, but I hoped they would have a different destiny, calmer, less troubled. But I don't want to bore you with my children, my grandchildren and their lives. It may be my fault, but I never tried to understand them. I wasn't really cut out for family life, I grew up as an only child. I loved them, naturally, but they didn't interest me very much. Did you have any children?"

"Yes, one, a painter. He's a very good boy, an artist. I was very close to my son, although I may have made him suffer—sometimes I was too strict. I used to criticise his work, I may have helped him less than other young artists. He didn't expect me to die like that, to leave him alone, without even a moment to talk to him and to tell him how fond I was of him."

My father had summoned us one Saturday afternoon at his home. We sat in the library. He was wearing a dark-blue dressing gown, he was pale and thin. He spoke about his cancer and his chemotherapy as though it were somebody else's cancer and chemotherapy. Then he explained—and his wife was also present—the terms of his will. He had prepared for his death with minute attention to every detail and he told me what I had to do to notify the rabbi whom he wanted to come and recite the Kaddish over his grave. This rabbi lived between Paris and Tel Aviv and I should have to organise his trip from Tel Aviv for the funeral. Then he gave me details about the undertakers I was to contact, and on how he wanted to be buried. He had even written down who was to be invited to his funeral.

I dined with one of Roland Topor's publishers, whom I had known since we were children, and he told me that Topor and Polanski had become friends at the Café de Flore in the early Sixties. He then spoke about Topor's father, Abraham, a Polish artist specialising in *naïfs*, who sold leather goods to keep his family.

"Did Topor earn a lot of money?"

"No, I believe he had had problems in these last few years, especially with the tax authorities. Of course, he made money with his drawings as well as with television and the cinema."

"Did he have many girlfriends?"

"Yes, he had lots. But the most extraordinary, the most irresistible thing I remember about him was his laugh, which was exceptional and contagious."

"Was he always drunk?"

"No, I think he drank more or less like all of us. He was afraid of doctors. He had a bit of heart trouble in his last years, but he refused to look after himself or get himself examined, and so he died, like a character in one of his surreal tales. Stupidity fascinated Topor just as it did Rabelais and Flaubert, and perhaps madness too. When we come back from our holidays, I must introduce you to one of his friends who can tell you a lot. I hadn't really seen Roland for several years. I went to his funeral. It was well attended. He was much loved."

When I went back to see my father's wife in the clinic, my sister came with me. While we were in the car, we wondered what could be done for someone so ill, who wanted to go to the clinic and then wanted to go home, who wanted the doctor and then hated him, who complained about her children to everyone. Was she really so desperate? What was the best thing to do?

At the clinic, we went up to her room. Unkempt, her eyes half-closed, she mumbled a few confused words, complaining that her sister had taken away her cheque book and that she couldn't leave …

I went downstairs to talk to her doctor who, in the usual ambiguous way of doctors, told me how we should behave, and what medication he had given her. He was an evasive man, who spoke to his patients one way, and to their relations in another. This double lexicon revealed a certain kind of common sense. According to him, we would have to wait for her to get used to the place and for the specialists to get used to her. When he went upstairs to see her, my sister and I stayed in the waiting room. While we were discussing how we should organise things, an old gentleman, bald, very clean, with a black vest and white shorts and black rubber shoes, came into the waiting room smoking a cigarette and holding a soft drink. He entered, went out, and then came back in again without his drink.

I asked him: "Are you a patient?"

"Yes, I'm in room twenty-two."

"Have you been here long?"

"No, just a month, but their results are miraculous, extraordinary."

"Are you suffering from depression too?"

"No, neither depressed, nor a drug addict, nor an alcoholic. May I sit down?"

"Of course, please do!" my sister said with a smile.

"You see, I've got a strange illness. I used to sleep twenty hours a day, I couldn't keep awake."

"Why was that?"

"I don't know, but now I'm all right. I wake up at eight in the morning. In actual fact, there was a reason. I'm bankrupt, I lost a lot of money. I had a little tailor's shop. In Tunis, before coming to Paris, I had a big tailor's shop and we had two maids. Now my wife can't even manage to find a job."

"But are you feeling better?" I asked him.

"Yes, I'm feeling very well. Thank God, I'm completely cured. The lady with you, is she your mother?"

"No, she's my sister."

"I'm sorry. I'm not good at faces and make mistakes about people's age."

"Thank you. We'll see you soon."

"Yes, when you come back, I'm in twenty-two. Everybody knows me here."

I went to lunch with my sister at The Flandrin, and we talked about how we should handle matters.

"What will she do this summer? Where will she go?" I asked.

"We'll see. We must be patient."

It was a sunny day, and hot, with a bit of wind. Paris in June is splendid when the weather is good and only a few white clouds can be seen scudding across the sky, and the air is sparkling. I was drinking a glass of cold white wine. The evenings are very long in June, and there's a violet light in the sky. Paris is my father's city, especially certain places, certain districts. I could see him dressed in blue, eating fruit: raspberries, melons, cherries, oranges. Years before, when I was a small boy, he smoked a pipe, after which he gave up smoking, and preferred to wear grey rather than blue. Certainly, if my father wanted us to remember him, he had succeeded. Since I was dealing with his wife's illness, and trying not to let things slide, I couldn't leave Paris, France, and the places and smells that made me think of him. I knew he was at rest now, in Montparnasse. Had his tastes changed, now that he was dead? Did Roland Topor make him laugh? Topor reminded me a little of a friend of my father's, Bouboul, a nickname coined because he was short and fat. He was a furrier, of Russian origin, who liked eating and drinking and frequenting the rich. He used to go out at night, he liked girls, and wore a heavy gold bracelet. I remember that when my grandfather died, Bouboul came to us for dinner and, despite our sadness, managed to make us laugh till we cried. My father liked to laugh, but he didn't do so very often, he took everything seriously. Life had to be precise and orderly as he felt it should be. And how did Topor view life?

It occurred to me that one person who had known him well was my ex-wife, and perhaps she might be able to give me some information. So I decided to phone her. I left a message on her answering service. I was trying to understand what sort of man Roland Topor had been, through his friends or people who had worked with him. But all I got was evasive answers; the people I spoke to would say, "I can't spare the time now, perhaps after the holidays."

"Yes, Roland was a very dear friend, but I'm just leaving. Perhaps you could call back in October … "

How come? What was hidden behind this artist? What was the secret surrounding his death? Why did a man who was so mild and kind, and penniless to boot, leave so much jealousy behind him in dying, so many people who claimed to have been 'the closest', 'the most important', but who preferred not to talk, not to compromise themselves? Why didn't they want to meet me, were they afraid of something? Was there a mystery, a secret, in the life or death of Roland Topor? Did he die a natural death? Had someone killed him?

In August, we all went away on holiday. Except for my father and Roland, who would never go on holiday or take a trip again. They would spend those weeks chatting away. My father might have told Roland the story of his last illness … During the last months of his life, he was working with a young industrialist from Lyons, and although he was prostrate with fatigue, in July he decided to go with him to Israel. He knew it was going to be his last trip to the country where he had been so many times and with which he felt such a strong bond. I asked him whether he wanted me to go with him, but he said no. He preferred to go with that young industrialist and, on his return, he said, "He was very kind to me, kinder than a son."

My father had also tried to wound me, my sister, my brother-in-law. I was fond of him, even of his cruelty, his need to be superior, his indifference. To say that my father made me suffer is to put it mildly. He made me feel wretched, incapable of managing my life decently.

I don't think that my father would talk to Roland Topor about his family, they were subjects of no interest to him. He had been an only child, rich and spoilt, and wanted to talk only about his life and his problems. I used to get bored with him, because he would always tell the same stories over and over, and he would tell them as though everything was quite extraordinary in comparison with the mediocre existence of others. I wonder if my father talked to Topor about money? Who knows if he found some way of criticising him, making him feel stupid about how he had spent it? But, after recounting their lives, loves and memories, what would Topor and my father talk about? What might they have invented, those two Jews—so different—always there together? Did they still have any relations with the living? Did they somehow continue to protect us? For them, the passage of time had changed. Probably, the souls of Roland Topor and my father were no longer in Montparnasse cemetery. In that place, only their decomposed bodies remained. Their souls may have gone to dwell in the body of a baby, or of a small child in some other part of the world. They're probably no longer Jews, no longer male, but they may have taken with them something from their former life—music, or a way of thinking. It can't be taken for granted, however, that reincarnation takes place immediately. A long pause is probably needed, during which the soul remains outside the body, regenerating itself. In that case, it's not true that my father and Roland will stay there for ever. Their bodies will putrefy, only a few bones will remain, and so they will no longer exist. There will only be their names inscribed on a gravestone. The lives of those who have passed on are recorded in their works and their tombs, the person merely becomes dust.

My ex-wife rang me. Her voice was sweet, but somewhat off-putting. I told her my father was dead.

She answered, "Someone told me, but I can't remember who. When did it happen?"

"Almost two years ago."

"Ah, I see. And your work?"

"Fine, I'm working a lot."

"I know you've written some successful novels and won a prize!"

"Success is a big word. I've written some books."

"My brother-in-law told me, he reads your books."

"I'd forgotten that you have a brother-in-law."

"And your sister?"

"She's well. She has become a psychiatrist. Her son is growing up."

"Have you remarried?"

"No, and you?"

"Neither."

"So I'm your only ex-husband?"

"So far, yes. Are you happy?"

"I don't know. What about you?"

"I'm all right. Life is pleasant. I'm even a bit tanned, I've just been to Provence for two weeks."

"Listen, I wanted to ask you something."

"Go ahead."

"Do you remember introducing Roland Topor to me years ago?"

"Yes, of course. It was at my Australian friend Mike's house."

"Was Topor a friend of yours?"

"Yes, I was fond of him, he was one of a group of artists I went around with, and still do."

"Did he die of a heart attack?"

"No, a stroke."

"He didn't expect it?"

"No, it happened quite suddenly."

"But did you know him well?"

"Yes, well enough, I told you."

"You know, I've found out that he's buried at Montparnasse, near my father. My father didn't like artists, and now they're there together, for ever."

"Well, Roland was a very nice man, cheerful, people liked him."

"You know, it's strange, when I ask people who knew my father to talk about him, they're quite happy to do so. But if I ask Topor's friends, or his son, or his publisher to talk about him, their answers are always evasive. They say something nice about him, and then shut up, as though there were some sort of mystery about him. I want to write something about my father and Topor, and can't find anything out."

"Invent it. Write what you like, whatever comes into your head."

"In order to write, I have to know."

"Or invent. It's not as if you lack ideas. It's been a pleasure talking to you. I shall be in Paris the whole summer. If you come, get in touch."

I thought that I shouldn't have spoken to her about Topor. After such a long silence, I had phoned her to ask for information about somebody else. I called her back to say that it had been a pleasure to hear her voice, and she replied, "Thank you."

I said, "I hope I didn't disturb you."

"No, but you didn't remember that I don't like talking on the phone."

In actual fact, I hadn't remembered. How old was my ex-wife? Almost forty. Eight years had gone by like the wind. She hadn't wanted to talk to me about Roland. She had hesitated, let fall little silences, pauses. Perhaps he had been her lover, perhaps they had made love. They might have got drunk together one night, there might even have been a quarrel, or a misunderstanding. When I asked her "Did he die of a heart attack?" she replied with the assured tone of someone in the know, "No, a stroke."

She told me, "If you don't know, invent!"

What could I invent about this artist? His father's name was Abraham, and he had an elder sister, Hélène, whom I'll look up in Paris. I know that, in the summertime, as a child, he used to go on holiday to Arcachon, in the Landes, where d'Annunzio lived in exile. I might add that the war years, when Roland was in hiding with his sister in the country, were like a film by Lelouch. I could say that Topor knew Milan, and had artist friends. There were more painter and sculptor friends than writers in his life. Perhaps because he had a more cheerful view of painting. He wrote that the painter "is devoured by his passion for his art". Then he says: "A painter is sad!" but, "Painters have to be sad". About writers, he wrote, "The writer weeps because literature is sad."

His friend Erik told me that it had been his sister Hélène, a lecturer and a serious-minded woman, who had particularly wanted him to be buried at Montparnasse, far from his parents, but close to other great artists. Hélène was enamoured of her talented brother who was different from her, less conventional, more fragile. Hélène believed she was respecting both the wishes of his parents, very proud of their famous son, and of Roland himself. Indeed, in one of his books, he had written a little poem that hinted at this wish. It went:

Au cimetière de Montparnasse,
parmi les tombes ordinaires,
il en est une sans carcasse,
où les défunts se désaltèrent.
On y est mieux qu'au bar d'en face,
les grands crus reviennent moins cher,
il y a toujours de la place,
et l'on ne manque pas de vers."

(In the cemetery at Montparnasse,
amongst the ordinary tombs,
there's one with no resident carcass,

it's where the deceased go to have a drink.
They prefer it to the bar opposite,
a good vintage costs less than you'd think,
you'll always find a space,
and they don't skimp on the verse.)

I know nothing about Hélène. I imagine her as a woman with a strong character, but with a certain sweetness. This is why I'm sure that in burying Roland at Montparnasse, she was thinking of that poem. He himself imagined being at Montparnasse, although not so soon, of course, since—as his publisher Bourgois says—he was terrified of doctors and illness. I felt that Roland and his sister were very close. He had great respect for Hélène. In one of Roland's books, there is a family photo showing them together, she already taller, he small, with the Eiffel Tower in the background.

Hélène was protective towards her brother. As a boy, Roland was thin, a chick with big eyes. Then he let himself go, with fast living and insatiable gluttony.

In this, he was unlike my father who was, on the contrary, rather prudent. At fifty, he stopped smoking, when he learnt that his secretary's husband had throat cancer. He no longer went skiing or played golf, because he felt too old. In his last years, he would fall ill in the winter, with bad influenza, bronchitis. He wore a blue scarf to protect himself from the cold, he who had always hated scarves.

I should have realised that his fragility disguised the disease that was devouring him.

THE FRENCH FATHER

I rang my father's wife at the clinic. She was better, back to her normal self, talking a bit with everybody, taking an interest in other people's doings. We remarked on the Italy-France football match. France had won on penalties, and Italy was eliminated from the world cup. She thought it had been a good match, played well. Football experts on the other hand were very upset, saying that Maldini was a terrible trainer, that Del Piero played badly, and so on.

I told my father's wife that two days earlier I had dreamt about her. We were at the seaside, in a big hotel, two large communicating rooms. She was on the terrace, wearing a black Olympic-style bathing costume.

"I've got a black costume, that's a fact!"

"You were happy, in an excellent mood."

"Thank goodness, I could really use that … "

On thinking about my father and Roland, two Jews but so different, two men who had respectively chosen order and disorder as the guidelines of their lives, I became aware that they did in fact have some points in common. Both had had parents who spoke French with a foreign accent, both had been devoted to their work and had sought to make it, to be successful. They wanted to be French, and to be acknowledged by their country as men of great merit.

What difference was there between my father's Alsatian parents and Roland's Polish ones? My grandparents would have been anonymous immigrants if they hadn't decided to live in luxury hotels, eat in luxury restaurants, and make their purchases in luxury shops. By so doing, they could frequent and—in some cases—become friendly with cosmopolitan people, expatriates, famous, honest and dishonest persons, whom they met at resorts, fashion houses, casinos, and who at that time crossed the oceans aboard transatlantic liners. My grandparents had lived within the confines of a world that gave them the illusion of shrugging off the melancholy or burdensome side of exile, the irritation of speaking French with a foreign accent. In the world of grand hotels and health resorts, everyone was a little bit foreign, everyone spoke with an accent. This is why, during the war, the world's adventurers and the desperate had taken refuge in New York, which had become their Mecca. In New York, having money was all you needed to enjoy an elegant life style.

I wonder whether my father and Topor were sincere in their talk. I think my father must have asked Roland, "Were you satisfied with your work? With your success?"

"No, not entirely, I should have liked more. I would have wished to be like Picasso, a name beyond dispute, an absolute talent, enjoying universal fame. I had talent, I worked hard, I don't think I wasted my time, but I'm aware that I'm not Picasso, and I have to say I'm sorry about that, it makes me suffer. I fear that if I had never lived, had never written or drawn, the course of art would have been the same. That is why I was not at peace when I died. I would have done better if I had followed my father's example. He painted, sculpted, but he also did another job to earn a living. He was the sweetest person, not an ounce of arrogance. I could have become a serious, respectable person like my sister, who has worked hard, taught, and in her modest way has had a good career. Of course, I should have liked to have more genius, more talent, no doubt. Do you understand? If I'd been like Picasso, you, although you are not interested in artists and the world of art, would have known who I was, without having to ask me. Isn't that so?"

"Yes, you're right. I didn't know who you were, whereas when I was alive I owned a picture by Picasso, that's true. But all the same, not everyone manages to become that famous. You could have had great talent and, if I had heard of you, I would have bought one of your pictures. But such things happen even in other worlds. You see, it's true that I was the President of the Jewish Community in France, the highest level a Jew can reach, but I wasn't a Rothschild, or a great man like de Gaulle! I had my own fears, my own laziness, and so I can't think I shall be remembered like Henry Kissinger or J P Morgan. We are alike, because we always had to be introduced, and tell other people what we do. Some people have no need of this, and they are the great. I must admit, I was middle class, and didn't want to lose certain privileges. I was a conformist, whereas you have to dare, be bold, unscrupulous, a bit of an adventurer and, above all, you have to have boundless ambition. Even with women, it's the same. In a certain way, I must admit, I'm afraid of them. You see, Roland, the problem boiled down to this. We made life too complicated."

"It may be true that Picasso was a Spanish immigrant, Joyce an Irish exile, but they had never been to America, they lived in a different way … Of course, if you had been Rothschild or Kissinger, I would have known who you were immediately and you wouldn't have had to add that you were President of the Jewish Community. If you had been Orson Welles, I wouldn't have needed to ask you whether you had made *Citizen Kane*, or whether you had married Rita Hayworth. But you must believe me, Mr President, it's not easy to resign oneself. I used to laugh a great deal and I had a lot of fun, but a part of me suffered, there's no doubt about that. I suffered because I wasn't well enough known in France. Maybe it's that particularly Jewish angst, an anxiety that is insecurity more than anything else. But from now on all we can say is, Roland Topor was that man and can change no longer. He can no longer hope to create an absolute masterpiece in the last years of his life. Old age was not part of Topor's destiny. That's how he had to die, and he had to be content with what he had been, for better or worse. I often thought, 'If I had drunk less, if I had gone to bed earlier, if I had been less of a wastrel, would I have done better things, produced more important works?' I don't think so. Creating a masterpiece is chance. Should I have preferred to be Van Gogh? Alone and wretched during the winters at Arles, torn by the violent light of the Mistral? I don't know. I've made many compromises, I've wanted many things. Even you perhaps, Mr President, couldn't have done more, because—in all sincerity—each of us is a victim of his own character, of his temperament, of his laziness. It's true that you weren't ambitious enough, or that you over-protected yourself."

"I wanted to be richer and more powerful, but my middle-class prudence prevailed. I was content to feel that

I had turned out very well in comparison to other people in my own world, or to others who had had a similar education. I never compromised myself, even in love. I didn't want to have problems, irritating situations. I have always sought to avoid direct confrontation, major disputes, grand gestures. I preferred to live somewhat hidden. Although my romantic temperament would have led me to escape, to break with things, my common sense always prevailed, keeping me bound to my country, my work and my wife. I must confess that my life gave me a lot of satisfaction, and I'm sorry that I fell ill and died so soon. I thought I would have lived longer. But that's how it went, I wasn't able to see the coming of the euro, celebrate New Year 2000. I don't know whether fate exists, or whether by being more careful one lives longer. Perhaps!"

I spoke on the phone with the publisher Christian Bourgois, who gave me an appointment for after the holidays, saying that he would give me the address of one of Topor's friends. I asked him if he knew his sister Hélène.

"I didn't know he had a sister. I knew his father, who became a painter in the latter years of his life."

I called another publishing house. For a month, I had been trying to phone a lady who had worked a great deal with Roland and knew him well. Her assistant answered.

"She's on holiday, but you can try this number tomorrow between five and seven, when she'll be passing by. I've already told her that you phoned."

"Excuse me, but could you tell me how I can get in touch with Roland's sister?" I asked.

"I wouldn't know. I didn't even know he had a sister. I never heard him speak of her."

Things continued to be elusive. I phoned the lady who had worked with Topor. She replied, "Yes I knew him well, professionally. He wanted to publish a book written by three authors: himself, his father and his son."

"Did you know his father and his son?"

"Yes, his father, Abraham, was an extraordinary man. You know that Roland worshipped his father. When he died, I remember, he was shattered, unrecognisable."

"Do you think Roland died because he couldn't accept his father's death?"

"No, I don't think so."

"Because he worked too hard? Smoked too much?"

"Oh no, that's all talk and no more."

"He was always unrestrainedly cheerful. One of his publishers told me that he had an extraordinary laugh."

"He had a happy life because he did what he liked doing. I don't know if he was really cheerful, or desperate, or if he was a mystic. He was a very elegant sort of person, never showed his suffering. He knew that laughter kills faith."

"But was he successful?"

"He was certainly a character. Lately, he had had some good results with the theatre, but in France, his humour and his fervid imagination put people off. The French are too rational. He was more successful in Germany, Belgium, Holland, in the northern countries, as well as in Italy, in Milan."

"And his son?"

"He loved him very much, and appreciated his work. His great love was his father, a formidable person, who was a naïf artist."

"And his mother?"

"He never spoke about her."

"And his sister?"

"I didn't know he had a sister. I'm sorry, but I can't stay on the phone any longer. If you like, we can talk again in September, after the holidays."

I returned to Paris. My ex-wife agreed to meet me in a café. She arrived like a ballerina, with white tennis shoes, tied-back hair, still-slim figure, big doe eyes, no make-up, no jewellery, grey T-shirt, black leather slacks and a light Chinese jacket. She drank a coffee, smoked several cigarettes, then ordered another coffee. She was happy to see me and surprised. I found her beautiful, despite a few white hairs. We talked about my book, her book, she asked about my love life, I about hers. I don't know whether there was any emotion, but there was tenderness. Then I told her about Topor.

"Nobody is willing to talk about him, so I did what you suggested. I used my imagination. No one knows he had a sister, for example."

"It's true."

"Did you know her?"

"Yes."

"Is she married?"

"I don't know whether she's still with her husband. I know she has children. I used to meet her every now and again with Roland."

"Were they very close?"

"Of course. And you, do you see your sister?"

"Yes, I'm seeing her this evening. What kind of relationship did you have with Roland?"

"I didn't belong to the inner circle of his closest friends. But for two summers, we found ourselves alone in Paris in August, and went out together every evening. This happened twice in seven years."

"Did you go to his funeral?"

"Yes."

"Were there really a lot of people there?"

"Yes, he had a great many friends. He was a much-loved person."

"Was there a rabbi?"

"No, he was Jewish, but he didn't believe in religion."

We went on talking about lots of things, about our lives. Then we embraced and promised to meet again soon.

Shortly after leaving my ex-wife, strolling along Boulevard Saint-Germain, I saw a gentleman with crew-cut white hair and a moustache, dressed all in black. I took a couple of steps back, and asked him, "Excuse me, but aren't you the publisher Pauvert?"

"No, I'm not. I'm another publisher."

"Please excuse me, I'm sorry to have bothered you, but I was thinking about Roland Topor, an artist and writer, who has just died, and I remembered that he used to work with Pauvert."

"That's right. I don't like—rather, I detest—Pauvert, but I was Roland Topor's publisher in the Sixties, as well as being a friend of his."

"It doesn't seem possible. I'm trying to understand what kind of person Roland Topor was, but I can't seem to manage it. People keep shutting the door in my face. If I ask what his sister was like, they reply, 'I didn't know he had a sister!'"

"It's all the same, you know. Besides, who gives a damn whether he had a sister or not? What's important is the man, himself, his work."

"It's strange. I began to get interested in Roland Topor because I discovered that he's buried next to my father in Montparnasse, and I found that extraordinary. My father, who hated writers, is buried right next to him, but they're such different kinds of Jews. But I imagined that being there, both dead, they'd end up becoming friends."

"Possibly they are. What's certain is that Roland's tomb is temporary. But what was it exactly that you wanted to know?"

"I'm trying to understand who Roland was, but I just can't manage to talk to anybody. I don't even know who he was married to."

"He had a girlfriend who lives in Rue de Grenelle, a big, well-built woman. Since he died, she got thin. I have an appointment now, but call me later on. I'll give you her telephone number."

"OK. I'll ring you about five."

"Fine. I should be at the office by then."

I called him at the appointed time.

"Do you remember me, this morning?"

"Yes, very well."

"Well, I should like to talk a bit."

"Where are you?"

"In a taxi."

"Ah, that won't do, you won't be able to concentrate, you're not calm. Let's meet on Wednesday."

"But I'm going back to Rome."

"Then call me from Rome, with some precise questions."

"Will you give me Roland's girl's number?"

"Yes."

I called. The girlish voice on the answering service was sweet, winning. In two days, I left several messages, but never got any answer. I knew that the woman's name was Marie. I didn't ask the publisher whether she lived with another man, whether she had suffered a lot, or how many years she had been with Topor. Was he a faithful type? Did he have more than one woman at a time?

I should have liked to meet Marie, talk with her, discover what kind of woman might have been attractive to Topor. She might be away for the Fourteenth of July holiday, in the country, or in the south of France. I seemed to gather that relations between her and Roland's son were not good, whereas she was on good terms with his sister Hélène.

The two deceased would certainly have talked about their parents, and Topor would have said, "You're lucky to be buried with your father and mother. Even if you never speak, at least you're close, whereas I'm alone, in a temporary tomb, although that's all right because everything's provisional anyway. But I should have liked to be near my father. I adored my father. It was essential for me to live with him, be at his side, talk with him very often, but now we don't talk any more, we shall never talk again, and I find that terrible. What's worse is that I couldn't bear living for long without him. He was the sweetest man, extraordinary, a great worker. He waited until his retirement for the luxury of being an artist!"

"Yes, I see. My father was a mild person, well-adjusted and strict. But the greatest laughs in my whole life were with him. In America, during the war, in the office. Of course, he was an old man with strong principles. He had fought in the trenches. They gave him a medal. During his lifetime he had to emigrate to America twice, but he always came back to France. He was an intelligent, up-to-date person. But he thought that France would have won the war against Hitler. Afterwards, he was quick to understand how things stood, and sent me to America ... "

"You must have a lot of money, because you always talk as though the world were tiny, as if you could stroll around easily between continents and cities. I've travelled too, of course. I've been to New York, I've worked with Americans, but, you see, I wasn't a rich man. Before dying, they persuaded me to write songs, which would have made me rich. Just think, rich! But that wasn't my fate."

"And your mother?"

"She was a dear woman, very dear."

"Mine was strange, tyrannical, very jealous, complicated. She always wanted me to be the best, the most handsome, the first, but she didn't help me. On the contrary, she made my life impossible. Nothing was ever enough, nothing was ever right for her. She gambled at the casino, was exaggeratedly fond of clothes, scents, food. She had a German accent, she was generous with her poorer relations and showed off the jewellery her husband gave her. She was a bit malicious, egocentric, she hated both my wives, and her jealousy was ferocious. I used to go and see my parents every evening, on my way back from work. We talked about everything, and were very intimate. Then they died, one after the other, and since they have gone I feel as though my memory is not as good as it was, so you must excuse me if I ask you something I have already asked you, but are you an only child?"

"I had a sister. We were very close, although different, but I've already told you that. You must excuse me, but today I feel tired, I don't want to remember. With you it's always a question of the past, of feelings. You're very much a Jew in that. You like going back to things, brooding over them. You didn't laugh enough and you took life too seriously, life's not like that. In actual fact, it is and it isn't. That's why I overdid my life, I put it to the test, I wore it out and pushed it as far as I could. Because I didn't really believe in it. And what's more, I died suddenly. I wasn't expecting it. It's better like that. Of course, I could have lived for another twenty years, and become more famous but that wasn't to be my fate. But it doesn't matter. I have drunk marvellous wines, made love with women whom I adored. But, tell me the truth, you never really had fun, never really let yourself go, did you? I don't think so. You wanted to be a worthy son, respected and important. And then, why do you always talk about your parents and not about your children, your grandchildren, your girlfriends? I'm sorry, but I'm a bit on edge today, I've got no patience, probably what I miss is a smoke or a glass of good wine. Naturally, here we can no longer do anything, just wait to be reincarnated somewhere in someone else."

"You're right. I'm a bore, but I'm not used to talking about my own affairs, telling things. My life has been wholly made up of secrets and lies, frustrations and shyness. I don't know why I was born handsome and strict. A moralist, cruel and intransigent. Perhaps it's because I was an only child!"

"You must stop thinking about yourself like that. You're no longer that person any more. You're not who you were. Now you're like me. A putrefying body and a soul awaiting reincarnation. So in the meantime you can relax and, above all, get out of that self that is yours no longer!"

"You're right, but it's not easy to change right away. When you die, it takes some time to detach yourself from your self. And then, although you're dead too, you were a younger man, with more enthusiasm, more energy!"

"Today I regret not being at my girlfriend Marie's home in Rue de Grenelle. I used to stay with her for hours, a blend of sleep, love and work. She was a sensuous woman, a bit fat, but I like them like that. I've always liked women with a bit of belly, big breasts, soft cheeks. It's nice to feel a woman's belly and breast. Now I should like to be in bed with her, lazily playing with her body, talking to her. The life of a dead person is too solitary. If you were a woman, it would be different. In love, the nice thing is the physical side, the bodily side, lust, desire, but also the seduction of words. Trying to win a woman with words, gestures, fantasy. I say this because I was ugly and bald. Judging by what you say, you were very handsome and seductive, so you conquered them another way. But now we're dead, I regret that you're here as my neighbour. Please don't be offended, it's just a manner of speaking, I've nothing against you, on the contrary! But just think, what if you were a beautiful fascinating woman? Being dead would be much less boring! Think how delightful it would be to have hours and hours of time, days, months, to try and seduce her, get her to fall in love. How wonderful! To be in the cemetery, just like talking in a café, trying to be interesting, letting our imagination work, imagining life together, trips, projects. Not even this was included in our destiny! As I no longer have a living body, I have no sexual drive any longer, so I don't miss sex, but I do miss pillow talk, intrigues, affairs, seduction. Do you see?"

"Yes, but now—if you don't mind—I'd like to be alone for a while. You're like a volcano, you're impetuous and, without realising, you move huge boulders, dormant memories and emotions. We'll talk some other time, I need some quiet."

In the meantime, I was in Paris for only a few hours. I had to go back to Italy. I was on the trail of Roland's girlfriend—I left her several messages, but she wasn't there and by now I was certain that our appointment would fall through. A pity, because she lived next to my hotel. While I was at the airport, my mobile rang.

"I'm Marie. I've just got back and found your messages."

"Yes. I'm sorry for pestering you, but I was just passing through Paris and wanted to talk to you, I hope you don't mind. I wanted to discuss Roland."

"I guessed you might. Go on!"

"I was looking for you because Roland and my father are buried next to each other at Montparnasse, and I am curious about Roland, his life and works, but I'm finding it very difficult to talk about him. I know he was greatly loved, and had many friends, but people are evasive, they don't want to tell me anything. The publisher Balland told me that after Roland's death, you lost weight because you had suffered so much!"

"No, if you see me, you'll discover that I've still got some flesh on me, but it's true that I lost four or five kilos, because I had no appetite."

"Were you living together?"

"Yes, at my place in Rue de Grenelle. We were always together."

"Just think, I knew nothing about you. I knew Roland had a sister, but it's impossible to find her, talk to her. Nobody remembers his sister. I learnt about her from a photo. Only his son and a sculptor friend spoke about you. I asked the sculptor why they hadn't buried Roland with his parents, and he said that his sister had preferred Montparnasse. She wanted her brother to rest near other great artists!"

"Well, to tell the truth, I agreed with Hélène. Roland must be in his rightful place. His son doesn't agree. Roland wasn't expecting to die, but his works mention Montparnasse cemetery several times and so I thought it might be a sign."

"That's true. I too have read a short poem of his that mentions Montparnasse cemetery. Anyway, I understand. What kind of person is Nicolas Topor? Did father and son get on?"

"Yes, they grew very close during his last year, after Nicolas got his divorce and went back to live in Paris. He's a thin young man, romantic looking; he's a good painter. Yes, Roland's father was a sculptor, and then became a painter."

"Did you know him?"

"Yes, he was an extraordinary person, highly intelligent."

"And his mother?"

"I never met her."

"Had you been together for a long time?"

"Two very intense years."

"What sort of woman is his sister?"

"Very different from him, shy. Now her brother's dead, her life has changed completely. She has two children, one of whom is very gifted, highly intelligent, rather like Roland. You should talk to him. Hélène's husband is African, but they no longer live together. I must leave you now, but if you phone me when you come back to Paris, we can meet up. Would you like me to give you Hélène's phone number?"

"Yes, thank you. Do you think I may call her?"

"She'll like that, she was very close to her brother. She'll be happy to know that someone's interested in her. Since Roland died, Hélène feels she's been left out. Now I really must go. Someone's ringing the bell."

"Then we'll be in touch?"

"Yes, I'm not going away any more."

The next day I phoned Hélène.

"Mrs Hélène Topor?"

"D'Almeida-Topor. Yes, that's me."

"I'm sorry to call at this hour. I don't want to disturb you, but Marie gave me your number, so I thought I would get in touch. I'm calling about your brother Roland, because I've discovered that he's buried next to my father in Montparnasse cemetery. The fact made me curious. I had met him with my first wife, one evening at the home of an Australian painter. She was a friend of his."

"What's your ex-wife's name?"

"Clemence De…"

"The writer?"

"Yes, that's her!"

"I can't say I know her well, but I saw her a couple of times with Roland."

"Was she a girlfriend?"

"That I don't know, but I don't think so, they were just friends."

"I've heard about you. I know that your brother was very fond of you, and that you had a very close relationship with your father."

"Yes, we've always been a close family."

"Your father was an artist too."

"Yes, a sculptor. An extraordinary sculptor."

"Did he make a living with his work?"

"No, when he came to stay in Paris shortly before the war, to earn a living he worked at the same job as his father had done in Poland—leather goods. When he retired, he worked only as an artist."

"How is it that Roland is buried in Montparnasse and has such a modest, almost temporary, tomb? Are you thinking of taking him away from there, and finding a place near his parents?"

"No, it's right that he should be in Montparnasse beside the other artists. When we've got the money, we shall have a more suitable tomb built."

"Why did he die poor?"

"Let's say he wasn't a rich man."

"Do you mind talking about your brother?"

"No, on the contrary, I'm happy to talk about Roland, but it's always difficult, painful, to think about someone who's no longer there, someone you've been close to for a lifetime. Roland was younger than me, but we were always inseparable."

"During the war, you escaped together to Savoy, if I'm not mistaken."

"Yes, that's right. We hid because the Germans were hunting for Jews. These are very old memories. If you wish, we can talk when you come to Paris next time. Phone me beforehand, and we'll fix a date."

"I'll do that. I apologise once more for disturbing you."

"You haven't disturbed me at all. It moves me to talk about my brother."

I felt rather dazed after the phone call. Roland Topor's life was beginning to invade mine and it seemed as though I had a parallel existence—one with my family, and one with his family. Roland and my father were resting quietly in their graves while I was talking about them with the people they had lived amongst. But did it matter to them? Not at all, because they didn't know and they had other worries. Perhaps I should put a stop to my interest in this story. I had listened to publishers, friends, his son, his girlfriend, his sister. That left only the nephew who they said resembled him. But, instead, shouldn't I have tried to talk about my father with his friends or with my own relations? Maybe there were many other things about my father that I didn't know and could have found out. The truth was different, though. I knew a lot about my father, but about Roland I still only knew that he was much loved by all and that no one wanted to tell me about him, creating an aura of mystery. Between the lines, I had understood that there was a little disagreement between Marie, Roland's last girlfriend, and his son Nicolas, regarding inheritance problems. Who did his drawings belong to? His paintings? His royalties? When it comes to artists, widows, lovers and children often quarrel over the inheritance.

Roland's work had been seized by the Inland Revenue and perhaps, as time went by, it might have become quite valuable. His son was dealing with this, but preferred not to make the value of his father's work increase in order to defend his own. Nicolas was not resigned to being just Roland's son and wanted success, he wanted to become famous.

What would I gain by meeting Marie, talking again with his publisher, getting to know his sister Hélène? Then what would happen? Would we become friends? I was fascinated by the idea of going to see Hélène at her flat, getting her to talk about Roland, about their childhood, their parents. About their life as children. What had they studied? How did they escape to Savoy? Had they been afraid of the Germans? Where had their parents been? And who were their parents' friends? Did their parents keep the Jewish festivals? Did his father fast on Yom Kippur, or wasn't he religious? What relationship had she had with her brother? It was going to be difficult to understand Roland's ties with other people. The fact that he frequently changed girlfriends meant that he didn't know how to love them; he was too egocentric. Had Marie, his last girlfriend, been important to him, had he truly loved her, or was she just one of the many, one of those younger, adoring women who surrounded him? And then, had he kept up close relations with Hélène? I could see that Roland was possessed of remarkable charm, and had been able to create a generous and exuberant character for himself, one that had left a deep impression. Among the persons around him, none had lived with such arrogance, with so many whims, so much indifference to the rules. In other words, he had defied society, its conventions and duties. Roland knew well that this attitude had cost him a lot, had caused difficulties for his career, put a brake on his success in France. But what a brilliant person! I had to pursue my research, to understand the man who lay next to my father.

His publisher had told me, "On his last night, I know that he went to Castel, the nightclub where he liked to celebrate, and stayed there till they closed at six in the morning."

"Did he go out every evening?"

"Almost always."

"But how did he manage it? Did he take drugs?"

"No, it was his nature. He drank only the best wines and champagne. Sometimes he would come to visit me at the publisher's in the morning, about nine or ten o'clock. I would just be getting down to work, he about to go home to sleep, and we would go and drink a glass of champagne in one of the bars. He was a generous man. When I used to go to see him, if I said, 'That's a nice drawing,' he would answer, 'If you want it, take it—it's yours.' Ah, Roland was a character! He worshipped his parents, his father, whom he also painted many times in his pictures. He was a small man, bald, with boundless energy. He used to travel around France with a suitcase full of leather goods. He used to say they sold better in the provinces. During the war, the children—Roland and Hélène—took refuge with some very Catholic country people, and it was in that bigoted atmosphere that Roland developed his taste for paradox and rebellion. His taste for mockery, for provocation. He travelled a lot, but was afraid of flying. The few times he went to New York, he travelled by sea."

"Why is it that his tomb is so modest? Is it true that his patrimony has been seized?"

"I saw to the funeral. The tomb is the way it is because we are waiting for a sculpture from a friend of ours, a talented Scandinavian artist who has promised to produce a monument for Roland, except that he's had too much work on his hands this year."

"Was his last girlfriend important for him?"

"He was a very sensual man. He used to fall in love, was very generous, but I would prefer not to talk about his love affairs, his women. Of course, he was a seducer, there's no doubt about that. He had many women. He used his charm to conquer them, his intelligence, his passion for things, for the work he was doing … "

"It is true that he laughed in an embarrassing way?"

"I don't know if it was embarrassing, but it was certainly singular. When he laughed in a restaurant, everyone knew that Roland was there. He was a great character."

"And his son?"

"He's a good person. Years ago I published a book of his drawings for children. Roland was very pleased."

"And money?"

"He spent a lot, he spent everything. He earned well, but money had no value for him. For that matter, not even his father knew how to manage money."

I spoke with Marie again on the phone. She told me she had written a small account of Roland's last hours. I asked her how long she would be staying in Paris, and we agreed to meet. Then I asked her where she was going on holiday.

"I don't know exactly. First I thought of Brittany, then Bordeaux. I might go as far as Provence, or even Spain. I'm going with my daughter."

"Is she Roland's daughter?"

"No, another man's. He's dead too."

"Are you going by car?"

"No, by train, boat, coach. We shall be away three weeks. We need a change of air. It's been a long cold winter."

I knew that Marie was blonde with brown eyes, she liked night life and her voice over the phone was sensual. I felt I wanted to continue the conversation.

"When did Roland work?"

"In the afternoons until six or seven, then he used to go out and his night life would begin."

"Was he always cheerful?"

"Perhaps, like everyone, he had his melancholic moments, and sometimes he got a bit tired of his frantic pace of living."

On my answering service, I found a message from my father's former secretary, asking me to call her at home, at any time. I called to find out what had happened.

"I took the liberty of calling you because I had a visit from your Aunt Micheline, your father's first cousin. She's in a bad way, she's desperate, she feels she's all alone in the world, she would like to get in touch with your family. I think she'll die soon. I felt very sorry for her."

"What can I do? Why doesn't she look up my father's wife, who's just come out of hospital?"

"Because they don't get on. Neither your father's wife nor his sister wants to see her. And so she talked with one of your children, who I think will come and see you."

"I don't see what my son has to do with it."

"He was the only member of the family here in Paris, and I can vouch for it that your aunt is in a very bad way."

"Tell her to phone me."

"May I give her your number?"

"Yes. Tell her to call tomorrow evening."

The secretary had been unctuous on the phone, an accomplice in an affair that made my flesh creep. I remembered that scheming old aunt, with long, reddish hair, a brown mink, a crocodile bag and a silk scarf round her neck. When my taxi arrived at the clinic in Neuilly-sur-Seine where my father was hospitalised, she was waiting for me at the entrance. Perhaps she had been told that I was coming. She came towards me, saying, "You poor thing, I'm so sorry!"

"About what?"

"Your father's death."

I recall not looking her in the face, as if trying to drive out her image. Nobody had the right to announce my father's death to me. I took the lift alone. Perhaps it wasn't true. But it was. I found my sister waiting for me, and we embraced. My father was dressed in his pyjamas, he was lying motionless on the bed. I had arrived too late. I hadn't seen him die. I stayed there alone with him. I wasn't sad, I didn't cry, I didn't really understand what had happened. I felt that I had to have the courage to stay in that room. Every now and then, I went up to him, caressed him. He was cold, but I hardly dared touch him, almost as though I were afraid of waking him, of disturbing him at that moment in which he was entering death, leaving his body. I gazed at him obsessively in order to try to stamp his image on my memory. I knew that when the medical staff came to take him away, I wouldn't see him ever again. They would cover him with a white sheet, they would lay my Taled over him … These were the last moments of intimacy, of solitude. I could no longer tell him anything, he no longer heard me, he could not answer because he was no longer there. But I didn't want to ask him anything, I just wanted to look at him, so as not to forget him. I was the last person to see him still lying on the bed, in his pyjamas, composed, with his hair combed.

The phone rang—it was Micheline, her voice agitated, anxious.

"What's the matter?"

"I feel all alone. I have no one any more, I need my family. I'm going to see your son. I'm so upset … "

I found her voice intolerable, and my thoughts returned to her long hair, her mink coat. I told her that if she needed, she could call me.

My son went to see her. When I asked him, "Is she really bad?" he replied, "I don't know. She was putting it on, of course. I don't want to go to see her any more, I never want to see her again."

"But is she really very bad?"

"I don't know. Maybe she is, maybe she isn't. She tries to make you feel sorry for her. I never want to go there again."

I recalled my father's grave, serious voice. Even when he was ill and lying on his bed, he would tell me his life story in solemn tones, the things he had done and said. He preferred monologue to conversation. He was a storyteller and he liked to charm his audience. Now he only had Roland Topor. He could tell him his story, or else ask him questions.

I can well imagine my father asking the man in the neighbouring grave, "If you had to summarise who you were in life, or how you will be remembered, what would you say?"

"A cloud of smoke."

"Come on, be serious. That's not what you think at all. You worked a great deal in your life."

"And if you stopped being serious for a moment? If just for once you were to tell me who you were when you were not the President?"

"But I'm not interested in knowing who I would have been had I not been who I was, do you see? I don't think of myself as President, but as an engineer. You see, my friend, imagination is a wonderful thing, it helps you to live, it's fascinating, but on its own it's dangerous. Believe me, it can lead to some terrible mistakes. An engineer, on the other hand, even if in a modest way, has studied in order to make earthly life more precise, more organised, more centred on certain parameters. Believe me, it's very important because in the long run, chaos and anarchy lead only to destruction and death. You see, my son's temperament is like yours, fanciful, something of a congenital liar, surreal, but I've always put him in a tough position, one in which he had to earn his living and—you can take it from me—it's done him a lot of good. I admit, the only thing an engineer can't solve are sentimental problems. But I'm verging on something too personal, and so I'll drop it."

"Not at all, please let yourself go, you can talk to me freely about your women. I have always loved women because they gave me a lot, embraces, abandonment. The most beautiful thing is to abandon yourself in a woman's arms. Better if you're a bit drunk, and your head's swimming. Don't tell me you don't know what it's like!"

"But I've never liked drinking, I hate drunkenness, turning one's back on reality. I think I have experienced love, however, the welling up of passionate love. But I've never allowed my passions to dominate me, I've never had the courage. You see, I believe that here at the cemetery, you and I are more or less equal, but not in life. Think of the difference between the lives of a person who saves and a person who squanders. It's not true that the person who saves has an easier life. You were a wastrel, ran up debts, had problems with the tax office, worries, you had to sell your paintings to pay those debts. But I had to save, so as not to damage my reputation as a rich man. I couldn't make mistakes, go bankrupt, diminish, get smaller, but it's not easy at all, there are contingencies when it's almost impossible to keep your head above water. And then, if you're rich, women only love you because you're rich and can offer them certain advantages."

"And if you're poor, it's the same. They may not be the same women, but then again, they may be. Women can love very different men, as you know. We may well discover that we have been loved by or have loved the same women. Pardon my presumption, but that's how it is! Then again, how do you know if a woman really loves you? But it doesn't matter. What counts is the illusion."

"I never had many love affairs. I got married twice, but most of all I thought about my work, my career, my money, sport. In short, what I can say is that as a rule I worked hard and tried to make a good job of what I was doing, that's all. I travelled a lot, though, I've been round the world several times. I used to go to Hong Kong, Japan, Brazil, the United States. I used to like being well dressed, I had a great passion for striped shirts, striped pyjamas, underpants, expensive dressing gowns, watches, and even cufflinks and pipes when I was younger."

"I used to smoke a pipe too, but I much preferred Havana cigars."

"I agree with you, they're very good. I used to smoke them in the early morning, leaving home. During the day, I preferred cigarettes, Winstons. Unfortunately, I'm convinced that that's where my cancer came from."

"I used to smoke a great deal and I died of a stroke, not cancer. It doesn't mean anything. Besides, we know nothing. But since you're so religious, you know that better than me. And while we're on the subject, let me satisfy my curiosity. Since your death, have you continued to pray?"

"I have to say that I never prayed much, even when I was alive. The only prayer I really knew—and since your parents were Polish Jews you know exactly what I mean— was the Kaddish. I used to recite it every day when my mother and father died, one only a few months after the other. I observed religious mourning and had time to learn that prayer by heart. I must say I liked the Kaddish, it gave me a feeling of belonging to the community. I was attracted by the fact that ten men had to be present to read it aloud twice a day, in whatever city I happened to be. Now I'm dead too and I can't say it because I'm alone, and even if you said it with me, we'd be two, three with my father and we might be able to count on my father-in-law, my second wife's father, who's buried here. But even so, we're only four Jewish men and we'd need another six. I'm sure that my children didn't observe religious mourning for me, they weren't as fond of me as I was of my own parents, a fondness that came from deep inside. Perhaps—although we can't see them—they come to the cemetery every now and again and recite a prayer, but it's not the same thing as religious mourning properly observed. But you're not a religious man and so you can't understand these things."

"I'm not, but I might have become one. I'm sorry I don't know anyone in this cemetery, because if I knew another six Jews, I would also be more than pleased to recite the Kaddish, even though I never did so for my own parents. It would be something new, to start praying, but it might be a way of passing the time. Intelligence and imagination are no longer of any use to us. There's no longer any point in trying to live in the fast lane, trying to bend the rules. I can't even feel sorry for myself any more. In praying, in reciting a prayer, there's something worthy. A man has to be humble before God, but there's something very intense, like very beautiful music."

"Were you married when you died?"

"No, I was living with a young woman, a blonde, taller than me, cheerful, we used to work together, we were always together. I went to live with her. The day I died I remember holding her in my arms. I was in a good mood because I had been up all night."

"However did you manage to stay up all night at your age?"

"It gave me the feeling of living more, exorcising a ghost, understanding more. You know, you tend to talk about yourself a lot, but there are many other things too. You think too much about your image, about your doings as a human being. But life isn't a manual of history and philosophy. I used to be fascinated by other people's tales, their ideas, their dreams and frustrations and then, as I've already told you, I adored the physical aspect, voluptuous and plastic, of women's lives."

"Yes, that's true, I do think a lot about myself, even though there's no point in that any more. I've never learnt to relax, to take advantage of life with serenity."

"To be serene, you have to be a bit of an idiot. How can you be serene when you know you have to die, that our situation is transient?"

"You're right. You have to be a bit stupid, irresponsible. But foolhardiness and imprudence can cost you dearly. I don't want to be unkind, but what did you leave your son?"

"My work, my works."

I was to meet Marie Binet at the Café de Flore at one o'clock. We asked each other:

"How shall I recognise you?"

I told her:

"I shall have a pencil in my mouth."

I got to Flore a few minutes early, dressed in a blue suit and blue tie with large white polka dots. She arrived about ten past one, dressed in black linen, with a white linen jacket and sandals with heels. I recognised her at once. We ordered two salads and two half-bottles of mineral water. She asked:

"Do you mind if I wear my dark glasses?"

"No, of course not. How is Roland's sister? I phoned her to find out whether I could see her, but she said that I had woken her up and that she didn't have time."

"She lectures in African Studies at the Sorbonne. She's petite, a very sweet, shy little woman."

"Is it true that she always quarrelled with her brother?"

"They used to insult each other. He would tell her that an observation of hers was stupid and she would get angry. But Hélène adored Roland, and Roland was very fond of her. They were inseparable."

"Did you see them often?"

"Yes, as long as Roland was alive. Then we lost touch."

"I tried calling his son Nicolas and left him a message. I hope I can manage to see him. I'm curious to see what he's like, whether he looks like his father."

"He's very shy, and doesn't say much."

"How did he get on with his father?"

"Roland used to tell him what he thought, without restraint."

"And he was shy. Was he afraid of his father?"

"Yes, he was afraid of him. But he's a strange boy. As soon as Roland died, he changed. He took charge of everything, from his works to his tomb. He wants to deal with it all, but he doesn't because he can't stand going to the cemetery, he can't handle that."

"Is he a good painter?"

"Let's say he has good taste."

"That's rather a cruel thing to say."

"Let's not talk about it."

"Was Roland strict?"

"No, he was anarchic, he could be argumentative."

"A gossip?"

"No, he used to say he had no time to waste. He hardly ever talked about other people."

"Why is it that the people who knew him are so mysterious about him? Why do they all behave like lovers claiming to be his favourite?"

"That's true. It's a bit like that. Roland absolutely wanted people to love him, so he tried to please whomever he was talking to. He was generous to a fault. He squandered his time, his money, and he offered everyone a drink."

"Did he drink a lot?"

"Yes, the best wines. He smoked cigars, cigarettes, a pipe. He always had to have something in his mouth."

"Was he greedy?"

"Yes, but for good things, he liked quality. But above all, he was incapable of dealing with the practical side of life. He hated reality. He used to behave strangely, didn't open his letters; he was afraid of receiving bad news, bills to be paid, or tax demands."

"Did he drive?"

"He had a licence, but said he didn't know how to drive. I used to take him around on my Vespa."

"What did he talk about?"

"Ideas. In the evening we'd go out, dinner would begin normally, then slowly the ideas would take shape and we'd talk until perhaps five in the morning. Then, when we got home, he'd rush to write them all down."

"With a pen?"

"No. I had given him a computer and he had got into the habit of using it to write very fast, as though in the grip of some sort of frenzy. He would listen to people, observe them. He was like his drawings, like his writing."

"He had a close friend, a Scandinavian sculptor."

"That's right, but it's a strange story. When Roland died, he promised to make a sculpture for his tomb. He wanted to sculpt an empty chair and place it on the tombstone, but I didn't see what it had to do with Roland. So I was against it. I'd like him to sculpt something that has to do with Roland, but I don't know how it's all going to end."

"Did you always go to Castel?"

"Yes, I remember that all his friends gathered there after the funeral and stayed for hours. It was as if it were one of our many late-night parties, but it was daytime."

"At what time was he buried?"

"In the morning, or perhaps it was afternoon. I don't remember. There was a big crowd, a lot of important people, and even a violinist. Some of his famous friends were there, all the people who in different ways had had something to do with him. Besides, even if he was anarchic, Roland was not averse to notoriety. He was like an actor. He could never have borne a banal funeral, he couldn't tolerate anything banal."

"Did he spend a lot of time making love?"

"We were always together. He'd had lots of women before me. He was faithful as long as the affair lasted, then something would snap ... But tell me about your father. Where is he buried?"

"In Montparnasse, beside Roland."

"It seems to me that instead of investigating Roland's life, you should be investigating your own father."

"I don't need to, because I know him well enough and can call up images, situations. He loved grand hotels, which he called 'palaces'. I remember him at Cannes, one summer, in one of the big hotels. We had a corner suite and my room was next to the one where he slept with his wife. I recall that he used to get angry with me because I would get up at night and go into their room. He slept naked, and I would go up to the bed and ask him, 'Dad, what must I do to get to sleep?'"

"One afternoon, we went to the tennis club to play together, and he didn't have white kit. He was wearing blue nylon shorts, a light-yellow sleeveless shirt, and dark-blue Dunlop tennis shoes. I remember my father would stay in bed, playing with me by tossing me an orange. He liked playing with oranges and fondling my head. I wasn't close to him and I hardly told him anything about my life. He always used to talk about his own, making it all seem extraordinary and highly adventurous."

"Roland was modest, he never used to talk about himself."

"Did he take a lot of medicines?"

"No, never. If he was ill, he stayed in bed and slept until it went away."

"My father, on the other hand, used medicines in his own peculiar way. If the doctor told him to take two pills per day, he would swallow four, thinking they would have a greater and quicker effect. He was forever talking about his many psychosomatic ills, which worried him. He kept having tests, consulting specialists, and then he'd get well before some other strange illness came along. I was amazed that a man who was so strict with himself and with others should indulge in talking about his various ills without any restraint. It was an attitude that was entirely in contrast with his need to feel that he was always elegant, impeccable … "

"Roland was vain in his own way, too. He would pretend he didn't care about anything, he didn't even know what shirt or jacket he had on, but in actual fact he was a dandy and loved luxury, there's no doubt about that. He was very loving, affectionate, like a child. I remember that when I organised the removal for him, he did nothing, he just sat on the boxes, reading old letters and weeping."

While Marie was speaking, I observed her. She wore her hair tied up and she had full lips. She was over forty, but looked thirty-five. Her armpits had not been properly shaved. I thought that Roland would have given her long kisses, he had found her sensual, joyful, he had liked her small childish teeth. Marie was a woman who wanted to have fun.

"Are you leaving for your holiday tomorrow?"

"No, I've changed my mind. I don't think I shall go away. I've been invited to Cortina, but I can't go. I never know why they invite me. I prefer going to Spain with my daughter for a week. I shall be back by mid-August."

"When shall we see each other?"

"After the mid-August holiday."

"Shall we sit in the sun for a while?"

"Really, I should be going."

My daughter had come to fetch me, and had heard part of our conversation. When we left Marie, Ginevra said, "She's very bohemian."

I didn't know what she meant by that 'bohemian'.

When I told Marie that Roland would have liked to be Picasso, she replied, "I'm sorry, but Roland wanted to be Roland, because he had a very high opinion of himself."

I spoke with his Italian publishers and they told me:

"When he came to Milan, he often stayed with us, especially if he had no money. We got to know each other in '68, which is when our long friendship began. He was afraid of flying, and if he came to stay with us in Sardinia, he used to take the boat from Corsica."

I thought about Marie having fun with Roland. She was fascinated by the life he offered her, but she wasn't in love with him.

I recalled that at a certain point in his life, when he was about forty-five, or perhaps earlier, my father, too, had been afraid of flying and for this reason had started travelling by sleeping car. I couldn't get close to my father because I was afraid of his reactions, the long faces, his punishments that involved burning all bridges, not speaking to each other. Whereas he claimed to be a cold man, he wanted to create passionate relationships all around him. I was a son he didn't understand. He neither understood what I did nor how I led my life. Every now and again he would summon Stefania, a friend who had worked with me for years, and ask her for information. She tried to reassure him on my account, but he didn't believe her, he couldn't accept having a son who was different from himself, he didn't believe I was an artist, he didn't want me to be Italian. Jokingly, my father called me 'the wandering Jew'. He didn't understand why I had no roots, no fixed address, why I didn't have a proper house, a wife …

In August I went on holiday to the United States and stayed in New York for a few days. I always feel at ease there, because everything seems simpler, less problematic. The fact of having a curious destiny, of being rootless, a 'wandering Jew', is normal there. What's more, I had lived the early years of my professional life in New York. My two children were born in that city, I wrote my first novel there, and there too, many times, I met my father. We would stroll around together, dine together. Perhaps we felt closer in New York, more equal, both of us in a foreign country. He became less French, I less Italian. It was a terrain where we were less sure of ourselves, where we had to make more effort. But even in New York we rubbed each other up the wrong way. I remember once on Madison Avenue, in front of a shop selling bags and suitcases, my father talked enthusiastically about the quality and the practicality of a dark-green nylon travelling bag in the shop window. I asked him, "Why don't you ever use those magnificent suitcases in the loft, the ones that belonged to your father?"

"Because I sold them, I sold all the useless junk there was in that loft."

"But there were also boxes with all my childhood books, and the ones I bought when I was at university."

"I don't know, they must have been sold."

I was astonished, but didn't say anything. I didn't dare say a word; in any case the books were there no longer, I would never find them again. It didn't even occur to him that this was offensive to me, a disappointment. What had been in that loft had been sold, and that was that. I could never oppose my father because in certain cases his injustice seemed to me so great that it reduced me to silence.

My sister joined me in New York and we went for a long walk in Battery Park. Looking at the Statue of Liberty in the distance, Yvonne said:

"Do you remember when I came to live in New York?"

"No, when?"

"Yes you do. With Mum and Dad when I was five. We came on a steamship called the *US Independence*, I remember it well. I was on the bridge and I saw the Statue of Liberty appearing in the distance … "

"And where did you stay?"

"In a hotel. I was forever watching cartoons on the television. It's odd, but in all those years, I never went downtown."

"Why ever not?"

"Dad never moved away from the few blocks between Park Avenue and Fifth Avenue around the hotel. And then, he never took me with him."

"Do you remember the boat trip?"

"Very vaguely. Mum suffered from seasickness and stayed in the cabin. I used to go and eat in the restaurant with Dad."

"And how did you return?"

"I don't know. I can only remember our arrival, which comes back to me now, on looking at the Statue of Liberty. What a strange relationship I had with our father. He and Mum lived in a world of their own … "

I could see that my sister suffered from some mysterious and inexplicable bond with our father. A man whom she had adored as a child, who had given her enormous security, and had then abandoned her. He no longer did anything for her, on the contrary, he put obstacles in her way. Yet the memory of that far-off Atlantic crossing, when she ate alone with him because they were the only two who weren't seasick, still revealed a great love, a poetic memory. The little girl who finally had her father all to herself.

I asked her, "Why didn't you come by plane?"

"Perhaps because there weren't any planes."

I remembered that those were the years when my father was afraid of flying and travelled only by train or by ship. My father's phobias made him even more singular in my eyes, different from all the others. The fact of having a father like that made me feel important.

Since his death, my sister and I had felt the need to be closer, to see each other more often. He had been our point of contact, but now he was there no more. For years, he had been alternately on good terms with me and angry with my sister, or, vice versa, angry with me and on excellent terms with her. It was as though he couldn't stand being on good terms with both of us at the same time. What's more, he preferred to see us separately, so that we never knew what he had said to the other.

My father had a love-hate relationship with America. He loved California, but wanted at all costs to be French, to speak French, and to pronounce foreign words with a French accent. To him, it was important to feel Jewish and French, decorated with the Legion of Honour.

When he was already seriously ill, I wondered whether I should ask his advice, whether he wished to make some suggestion about my life, but he didn't say anything much. He spoke about himself, about his parents. It was implicit that there was no need to reproach each other with anything, or to talk about our mutual disappointments. That was how it went. My father was never to know many things about my life, nor I about his. We were to take leave of each other on good terms, but surrounded by an aura of mystery. Excessive familiarity was not part of our rules. In any case he was my father and I was his son. He always wanted to be serious and never let his hair down. He never touched on intimate subjects, never attempted to find out whether others were happy or not. Happiness was a subject that didn't concern him, because his life had been built on ambition, not happiness. We never spoke about his fears or weaknesses, nor about his feelings, his fragility, his sorrows. Nor did I confide in him. We made conversation. He was content with his intelligence, his deeds, his memories, with talking about people he had known, and the times when he had played the leading role. He hated verbal clashes, raised voices, direct confrontation, disputes. He was curious about intellectuals, of whom he knew many, but he surveyed them from afar, like a race of people who were necessary, but very different from him. To be treated as a son by my father meant:

"That's your problem, sort it out. You chose an absurd and arrogant profession such as that of a writer or journalist, and that's your business. You chose to live in a dishonest and provincial country like Italy, you chose to write in a language like Italian, which nobody understands; well, that's your business too, you deal with it. You're over forty and you haven't even got the lowest grade of the Legion of Honour, you should be ashamed."

When I talked about my work, he would listen, but it bored him. I frequented circles he knew nothing about, and that didn't reassure him.

I don't know what kind of father Roland Topor was, I shall talk to his son about it when I meet him in Paris. But the Topors, more or less successful, and in a more or less eclectic fashion, were all painters: grandfather, father, and son. Theirs was an artist's life.

My father would have preferred me to work in industry, in commerce, or in banking, a serious and profitable job like his own, with work, leisure, and holidays all cleanly separated …

What did Roland and my father talk about, when I was in New York, thinking about them? Roland probably said:

"You see, there's no one here, only foreign tourists, who come to pay their respects to certain well-known figures. Seeing that my family still hasn't decided to solve the problem of my tomb, this rather anonymous looking stone doesn't attract anybody's attention. What's more, I don't think that my name has yet been officially included in the cemetery brochure with the other famous names. It's a pity my son's so shy, and my sister so indecisive. But I'm certain she'll manage to get her way in the end. After all, my success was important to her, she was proud of it—even though my success can't be compared to that of the other illustrious men buried here."

"Roland! You're incredibly vain and narcissistic!"

"Yes, I am. I don't want the place due to me to be taken away! We've already said that I'm not Picasso, but that doesn't mean much. What's more, the world's changing. Picasso was an idol, an icon, but nowadays that kind of personality cult no longer exists, even in show business. Tell me the truth, do you think anyone has managed to replace Edith Piaf, Yves Montand, Elvis Presley or Frank Sinatra?"

"I don't know. I don't know much about certain things, they don't interest me. I thought you were more detached, above fame and gossip. But if what you miss are German, Belgian or American tourists coming to place a flower on your grave, believe me, you disappoint me a little. So what should I say, then, after having occupied positions far more prestigious and important than yours, and never having run up debts in my life, I, who have always been a respectable person, about the fact that besides my family—and I don't even know which of them—nobody will ever come to visit my tomb?"

"It's not the same thing. I am an artist and if I'm not remembered, my work will disappear, and I don't know whether I can trust my heirs."

"But whoever said that you have to trust your heirs or your girlfriend! Believe me, your attachment to your fame—which I should define as lower middle class—disappoints me!"

"Good for you! You accuse me of being lower middle class, because you know that no one will ever come to visit the tomb of a man who has not left any works behind him! It really irritates you that people will remember an artist like me, who led an irregular, disorderly and absurd life, when they won't bother about someone who has led a serious upper-middle-class life, made up solely of duties and responsibilities. So I should stay in a corner, punished and forgotten. Oh no, dear Mr Elkann! My drawings and pictures are on show in museums. My books are reprinted, my plays are performed. But, just a moment, I'm sorry, I didn't mean to be aggressive with you, start on the class struggle, or make comparisons as to which of us was better or led a more proper life. After all, you lived twenty years longer than I did! Just think what I could have done in twenty years. But now we're dead, we're here, so let's try not to quarrel, show understanding, friendship. And for God's sake, even if we have some weaknesses and vanity, what does it matter, we're dead!"

"Yes, that's true. While the others are on holiday, we are dead, what bad luck! When you're alive, you don't notice how beautiful and fascinating life is, and how you can ruin your life by putting up with worries, sorrows, and problems, which then disappear. Here we no longer have anything to worry about, neither moving house, nor insurance coverage, or getting dressed or going to the barber's, or saving money, not even whether we're doing well or badly. You're right, what use is quarrelling, boasting of our former qualities? Instead, we can talk calmly. I was not a very cheerful man, I admit. I was afraid, I didn't trust anyone."

"I don't want to think any more about what I did before. I don't even have a sex drive any longer, so I don't feel alone any more without a woman's embrace. I died in a woman's arms and now I'm talking with you. I must confess that I'm not bored. I don't know whether it's day or night, whether I'm asleep or not. I'm not even tired any more. I'm calm, and that never happened to me before."

"I can understand that for you tranquillity may seem boring, difficult to bear. Living without being in love is like not living, but in actual fact our real punishment—and we must resign ourselves to this, dear Roland—is that we are dead."

"It's true. We talk and talk, no longer knowing what talking means, to no end."

"That's right."

While I was in New York, I occasionally thought of my father and Roland. I felt guilty, because I was still alive, I could travel, move about, see a lot of people, whereas they no longer could. I felt that being far away from Paris, from their graves, was a kind of betrayal. And my thoughts often returned to my father, I felt his absence, I knew that I couldn't phone him, tell him what I was doing.

When he died, my mother didn't say anything to me. I went through my mourning in silence. I don't know why my mother harboured so much resentment towards my father, I don't know what happened between them, but I was always distressed because they didn't have faith in each other. I don't know what impression my father's death made on my mother. She didn't tell me. I would have liked her to go and meditate before my father's tomb. Instead, she stayed holed up in Turin, or in her country house, which was the most important thing to her, because it reminded her of her family. It's strange that my parents thought far more about their own parents than they did about their children. I know that, out of kindness, a sense of duty, my mother had telephoned my father when he was ill, but relations between them remained cold. I was born to them when their marriage was almost over, so that I had to spend my childhood and adolescence between two worlds without peace, without my home. Always on the point of departure, waiting anxiously for a phone call. I was a disappointment to my father and my mother because I didn't study the way I should have, because I never chose what they considered to be the right path.

In what way do I feel my father's absence? What is a father when he's no longer there? Does becoming a father mean that no one consoles us or loses their temper with us any more, that no one is our boss any longer, or our best friend? Does it mean that our life is no longer unlimited? In just a few more years, we too shall grow old and die. I have been left alone and I must go on. Often, when I face a decision I have to make, I wonder what my father would have done in my place, what advice he would have given me. When he was alive, I rarely listened to his suggestions, but now he's no longer there ... Sometimes I don't know who to turn to, I have to do things alone, find the energy in myself. One becomes aware that one's children can't replace one's parents. You can't say the same things to them. You can't be weak with your children, you can't ask them to console you. You have to give them reliable information, guide them, advise them, help them and above all make them talk about themselves—always and only about themselves. That's the way it is, we didn't help our parents either and what we miss is that they're no longer here, ready to listen to us.

Nicolas Topor chose a brasserie at the Opéra for our first appointment. He told me he would be wearing a red shirt so that I could recognise him and if it was all right by me, we could meet at one o'clock.

I arrived early for the appointment. I imagined Nicolas as small and frail, with a beige raincoat and a tomato-red shirt. Nervously, I went in and out of the brasserie where we had agreed to meet, yet I couldn't see him. He was late, or had changed his mind, or had made a mistake about the day. At a certain point, I saw a loose-limbed young man with a long neck, very full red lips, large, light-coloured slightly bulging eyes like Roland's, small wide-spaced teeth, and sleek black hair. His expression was kind but absent. He was dressed like a French artist, but had the air of a foreigner, someone just passing through. He could have been an actor, but in a black-and-white film. The manager of the brasserie asked us whether we wanted a table for smokers or non-smokers. It was all the same to me, Nicolas was undecided and then chose a corner where smoking was allowed. We ordered some food and he very carefully chose a red wine from the Loire and asked for a packet of cigarettes. When the wine waiter brought the wine, Nicolas tasted it competently, and gave his approval with a smile.

In order to break the ice, I asked him, "Do you like wine?"

"Yes, my father taught me about wine culture."

"He drank a lot, didn't he?"

"Yes, good wines, and always in company. When he was alone, he drank tea."

Meanwhile a girl had come with the cigarette tray. Nicolas chose a packet of Philip Morris. I knew he had been diffident about our appointment, but after the first glass of wine, I became aware that he was warming up and was in a good humour. So, a few minutes later, he said, "I'm sorry I was so evasive and aggressive with you the first time you telephoned me, but I was too upset. You see, my father's death took me by surprise. It was a terrible blow to me."

"Was he ill?"

"No, I don't think so, but he didn't look after himself. He was afraid of doctors. His life had become excessive, he was tired, exhausted. On the very last day we met, the day before he died, I thought he was very much on edge. I guessed something was the matter. He lived next to me. I know that he spent his last night pub crawling with his friends, then the day after he had breakfast with a publisher to whom he had to give some texts. Then he went home, we talked to each other on the phone. He told me he had an appointment and would call me back in a couple of hours. I had got down to work happily when the phone rang. It was someone who had gone to visit my father, who told me he had lost consciousness. Could I come immediately? By then he was in an irreversible coma."

"Was he a difficult father?"

"Yes, at times even severe, exacting. He helped young people, he liked the role of teacher, but he didn't do it with me because I was his son."

"And you were jealous?"

"Sometimes, yes, very. I wondered why he didn't want to help me. But in his own way he did help. I never understood why he couldn't accept my first marriage, my two children."

"Didn't he want to become a grandfather?"

"No, but then he got used to it."

"And with your mother?"

"It was a love affair that lasted two years. But it was impossible, even as regards relations with their respective families. My father's parents and my mother's parents couldn't stand one other. My mother came from a family of Polish nobles and Russian Cossacks, while my father was the son of an artist, a Polish Jew. What's more—but you should ask my aunt about this—during the war, my father, who had fled to stay with folk who lived in the countryside, had had to wear the yellow star."

"Your father had a great passion, a great love, for your grandfather. Did he respect him a lot, did he fear him?"

"Yes, in a certain way he did. They were very different. My grandfather was more of a traditional painter, more disciplined. He ate simple food which he cooked himself. He drank only two glasses of claret a day. Whereas my father always ate excellent food, drank a lot, and kept unholy hours."

"Did that worry your grandfather?"

"I think so. I think that my father's continually excessive lifestyle bothered him, and his sister, too. My aunt even thinks my father committed suicide. But they had a very special relationship. She was older than he was, had always protected him and thought he was a genius. Unfortunately, in France they don't give my father the recognition he deserves as an artist. Since he died, there have been requests for exhibitions in Germany, Holland, Belgium and Italy, but not in France. He had always been provocative, an anarchist. He refused decorations and then he had problems with the Inland Revenue, he hadn't paid his taxes."

"And women?"

"He liked women younger than he was, delicate, uncertain about life. He liked to play the Pygmalion. But being his girlfriend can't have been easy because he demanded that they pander to his whims and accompany him everywhere, without ever arguing. He would spend whole nights drinking, talking with people, sometimes he would make a sketch, take notes. Part of his inspiration came to him that way. He had enormous creative energy and he did only what he wanted, no more. But then, I too wanted to become a painter, just a painter ... It's costing me a lot, but never mind!"

"Was your father happy for you to become a painter?"

"Yes, he followed my work and was quite severe, as I said earlier."

"What sort of relationship did he have with your girlfriends?"

"He never liked any of them, except the one who became my second wife. It was he who introduced us."

"It's odd that our fathers are buried beside each other. My father was quite another kind of man, with whom I had little familiarity. I was afraid he'd forget me, that he'd cancel out his affection for me. I sensed no solidarity in him. I knew he wanted me to be different and I had to hide whatever counted for me. Only at the end did he accept the life I had chosen. Perhaps because he was too weak, too ill, and needed my affection."

I got the impression that Nicolas wasn't curious about my father, had no interest in him. He didn't want to know who he was, but he was starting to like me. He said that we could meet again, and he showed me photos of some of his pictures and a small book of drawings illustrating his father's aphorisms. He asked me where I was living, and we exchanged addresses. The conversation flowed smoothly. I felt that Nicolas was mild, determined, discreet ...

I asked him, "Do you miss your father a lot?"

"A bit less. I'm getting used to it. I've got my children, my wife, and then, I've got his works. He used to read a great deal, he was a very cultivated man. He left me his library and, every now and again, I take up a book, leaf through the pages, and find that here and there he had made notes, tiny drawings, sketches. I'm dealing with his works, but I mustn't lose sight of my own, of my own identity as a painter ... I hope you can come to my exhibition at the end of November."

"Yes, I'll try to come back to Paris, I should like to meet your aunt. She's the person who knew your father best."

"Let's say that they spent all their childhood together. My aunt's point of view is not objective. Her brother's death was a terrible blow to her."

"Do you see her often?"

"Every once in a while, as I said, I have to think about my work, my wife. And you yourself live in Italy?"

"Yes. I know that your father had a lot of friends in Milan."

"That's right. They understood his work, and they also enjoyed his company. I know them quite well, too. But if you're living in Italy, you should go and see them. They know a lot about my father."

"I shall have to leave you now, because I'm starting the Kippur fast in a few hours."

"Well, don't hesitate to call me when you come back. I shall stay on here to finish my glass of wine, if you don't mind."

I caught a taxi at Place de l'Opéra, thinking that Nicolas was a nice, shy person. He looked a bit like Chopin, or some Russian nobleman, some fictional character. He lived in his own world, in his dreams, and in the memory of his father. I didn't know if we would meet again, or when. He didn't want to know the more intimate details I was trying to find out about his father. He didn't want to judge him. It was clear that, for him, he had been a strong, intrusive presence, but now he was seeking his own personal identity, far removed and different from his father's.

I had an appointment at the Trocadéro with my nephew Edward, a reserved boy of thirteen, shy, slim, well-mannered. We went to the synagogue together, he sat in my place, and I in my father's. He had never been to the synagogue, had never worn a Taled, but the atmosphere of prayers and chants fascinated him. He wanted to know if I would recite the Kaddish, and when I did so I saw that he was proud of me. In giving him my blessing I thought back to when I was his age, and was skinny and shy like him, sitting beside my father, with the same people around, who greeted us and talked to us affectionately. There, we felt we had a tradition and a history and were moved when the Grand Rabbi of Paris, a distinguished man with a bushy white beard, recalled my father who, according to him, had given an important stimulus to the cultural and spiritual life of the Community. The synagogue was my father's world, his people, those to whom he devoted most of his time. For years he had gone there to pray, to talk with other men, to solve problems. After his parents' death, it was there, in that synagogue, amongst other Jews, alongside the Rabbis, that he had found the focus of his existence. At bottom, my father's appeal derived from the fact that he was a shy man, and also a very spiritual one. I believe he had a close relationship with God. In his solitude, he often used to think of religion, philosophy. Probably he would have liked to be an Orthodox Jew, but circumstances were against it.

I must admit that on that day of Kippur at the synagogue, I felt less alone, closer to my father, and to our traditions. Sitting there in the temple with my nephew was like ensuring that my father and his traditions would live on. It seemed as if he were there with us and that the whole day of Kippur was dedicated to him, as always, in the same way, in the same Community, among the same people. Time stood still. This is the fascination of Judaism, the repetition of gestures, prayers and rituals through the millennia.

THE FRENCH FATHER

The day after Kippur, I had an appointment with Hélène d'Almeida-Topor, Roland's sister. I didn't know how she would treat me. I hadn't attempted to imagine her physical aspect. She received me with courtesy at her office, not a large room, with two desks facing each other and many shelves full of books. She asked me to sit down. Hélène is a small woman, with thick reddish hair cut in a pageboy style. Seated at the opposite side of her desk, she looked me in the eyes and I felt as though I were in the dock. We spoke about her work, her life in Africa, her nephew, the war years.

"My brother and I wore the yellow star."

"Were you afraid?"

"No, children don't think about death. When my father managed to escape and we knew where he was hiding, the concierge's wife tried to make us talk so as to report him to the Fascist militia, but my brother—who was not even four at the time—and I didn't talk. Afterwards we took refuge with some country folk. My brother has always drawn, ever since he was a child."

"Did he know he'd become a famous artist?"

"Yes, in a certain sense he did. When he was about sixteen, he said that he intended to leave school and my mother and I were against it, but my father encouraged him to go to art school. Then, at eighteen, he immediately set out to make a name for himself, and he had his first exhibitions."

"Didn't he lead a rather excessive life?"

"Perhaps it was excessive, but it depends what you mean … "

"He was a night-bird."

"At home we've always been night-birds, particularly my mother. She used to wake up late and we couldn't use the telephone during the morning. My father, on the other hand, used to get up early; he was more meticulous, but perhaps that's not the right word."

"More responsible than his son?"

"He was, in another way. My brother was a responsible person, only he couldn't bear to do things he didn't like."

"You see, I wanted to talk to you about your brother, because the fact that two such different Jews are buried together has made my father's death less sad."

"My brother was, of course, a Jew in a certain sense, but we weren't religious, not even believers. Not even my father was. Sometimes he used to speak Yiddish with my mother so that we couldn't understand, and would read a Yiddish newspaper, but it never mattered to us at all."

"Indeed, whereas it was extremely important for my father. He was the President of the Jewish Community."

"We were not religious, we never spoke about religion."

"It was you who wanted your brother to be buried in Montparnasse, wasn't it?"

"I wasn't the first one to have the idea. It was Marie—his girlfriend—because he was writing a libretto that was set there, in that cemetery. But I wasn't against it, not in the slightest. But he wouldn't have been against it either."

"Why? Would he have been happy to be buried among other famous artists?"

"I don't know. Perhaps he would. What's more, he deserved it!"

"But I know there have been problems about the tomb ... A sculptor friend of his wanted to make a sculpture, but Marie was against it, or something like that."

"No, it wasn't Marie, it was me. I don't want someone else's sculpture on my brother's tomb, an empty *bistrot* chair. It's true that my brother loved the *bistrots*, he loved going there with his friends to drink and talk, but there was also another side to his character, a deeper side, an important inner and intellectual life. I don't know why I'm telling you this. But I do think that if there is to be a work of art on his tomb, it should be one of his ... "

"I imagined that Roland and my father might talk together, in a certain sense maybe even become friends."

"Yes, I see, although I think it's improbable that two dead men could talk to each other. I don't believe in the soul—death is the end of everything."

"But you still have his works, Roland's books."

"Of course. In our family, we're not interested in material things, houses, inheritances. What counts are the works one leaves, and I think that Roland's work will endure. My father made small bronze sculptures because he thought that bronze would last over the centuries like the earth itself."

"Did your brother envy great artists like Brâncuşi or Picasso?"

"No, absolutely not. He felt he was a great artist, and I sincerely believe he was. Unfortunately, they made his life more difficult here in France, because he was insolent, because he refused decorations, because he didn't want to pay taxes."

"And what were his relations with women like? You have known them all, haven't you?"

"Yes, many of them, and they were excellent relationships too. The women he loved became friends of mine, but he always chose them young and so they ended up by leaving him."

"Did that make him suffer?"

"Yes, but he found consolation in his work."

While she talked, Hélène made elegant gestures with her hands, or rested her cheek on the palm of her hand. Her eyes were darting, watchful. At times, she laughed heartily. In short, like her brother, it was clear that she was fond of laughter, even if her laugh was more restrained. She was glad to talk with me about Roland and her father, even though she found me morbid when I asked her for too many details. I realised that Roland really was Hélène's dearly beloved brother, the little big man of the family, but one who made her despair because he didn't want to pay his taxes.

"My father was worried about Roland, because he wouldn't face problems. That's how my brother was, he understood everything, but tended to be indolent, tone things down, be evasive. That's why he always neglected his health, or held money in contempt because you could always find it one way or another, there was always someone who would buy a drawing or a poster. Italian and German collectors would come and give him bags of money, but instead of paying his taxes, he would invite his friends to eat and drink at the best restaurants. Those were extraordinary evenings and nights. Even I used to stay up late every now and again for those dinners. Roland liked having me around. You can't understand my brother's character if you don't know about his mad, infinite, absolute generosity. He was very kind, affectionate in a unique way, even with my children. And with my father!"

"Did he have heart problems?"

"He wasn't ill at all, he didn't go to the doctor's. If he had been ill, he would have gone, because he was a hypochondriac. Just think, an Italian paper even said that Roland had cancer! No, that's not true at all, he had a stroke."

"And how did you learn about it?"

"Just imagine, I was in Istanbul and had talked to him the day before. He gave me suggestions about what I should see. We finished our conversation in the usual way. He always asked whether I needed anything, if I needed money. I always asked him whether he was all right and he told me he was."

"Was he a genius?"

"Of course he was, he was extraordinary. He was incredibly cultured, and he told me what books I should read. Roland used to read anything and everything, voraciously."

"When?"

"All the time. When he wasn't working, he read. He was very interested in a wide range of different subjects."

"You know that I am writing a novel about my father and your brother and, for the purposes of the book, I would have preferred it if you had slammed the door in my face, told me you had nothing to say, and that I was indiscreet."

"If you want to write a novel, write what you like. Write that I insulted you, that I wouldn't let you into my office, that I'm a dreadful woman. Are you sure you wouldn't like to go to the café? I would willingly offer you a cup of tea, a coffee, or a whisky. I'm sorry, but I have nothing in the office. Novels nowadays seem to have neither plot nor plan. So you can say whatever you want. I didn't understand why you wanted to see me, what you wanted from me. That's why I was undecided whether to see you or not, but you're a nice person, so you can come to see me whenever you wish. I like talking about my brother. I almost never talk about him now, almost never see his friends or girlfriends."

"How are your relations with Nicolas?"

"Very good, we're very fond of each other. He's a loveable young man, but he's not my brother. You can understand what it means to spend your life with someone, and then he's no longer there!"

"I can understand that very well. Don't you think he and my father might talk together, make friends?"

"In actual fact, or in your novel?"

"In reality."

"That sounds crazy to me. In reality, the dead don't talk, but in your novel it may be a good idea. Why not!"

"So, are you encouraging me to go ahead with my project?"

"Yes, I am. If that's what inspired you, go ahead!"

"I'll get you to read the manuscript."

"That won't be necessary. I'll buy the book when it comes out."

We laughed while Hélène Topor, a petite, affectionate woman, full of contrasts, feelings and passion, accompanied me to the lift.

"Good luck with your work. I hope to see you again soon."

Walking through the streets of the Marais in the rain, I puzzled over what had happened. For months I had been imagining what Nicolas and Hélène Topor were like, wondering how they would have treated me, what they would have said about Roland and, as usual, reality was less inspiring than the dream. They were two kind, affectionate people, left alone after the death of Roland, who had occupied an enormous place in their lives. His sudden death had left them surprised and shaken. Long months of silence had followed, until I came along and broke the ice, making them talk once more about Roland, who had always been their favourite subject of conversation. That exceptional and unpredictable man had kept them on tenterhooks for years, had amused them and made them dream, had scared them and dragged them along on his nightly sprees, his flights of fancy, and his excesses.

Now they were back with their ordinary, organised lives, with no excesses. They were left with memories and back taxes to be paid. Roland had left them many tasks to perform. They would have to organise exhibitions, conferences, but he would no longer be there with them; he was with my father in Montparnasse cemetery. There, he was getting used to the tranquillity of death, to the fact of having to stay in the same place with the same neighbours. He no longer needed even to dream or to laugh. But Roland and my father still had the urge to chat together. My father said to him:

"You see, Roland, I'm very glad that you're here. Talking is the only thing left to me, and with you I feel free to say things I have never said to anyone during my lifetime. I didn't trust other people and was obsessed with defending my image. Having an image is important, because it protects you, but it's very wearisome. Staying handsome and slim means giving up sweets, wine, cheese, pleasures. And then the will power, the effort, the example you try to set your children. You see, after I had been here for a bit, I felt a great peace within me. I no longer needed to push myself, look at my watch, wonder whether I was losing or winning, whether I had done everything I should have done. To tell the truth, the only thing I regret is not having been buried in Jerusalem. I should have liked to be there, beneath those walls, in the country that was so dear to me, where I felt happy. Unfortunately, I never had the courage to drop everything and go over there for ever. You see, wherever I've lived, I have always had a longing for somewhere else. It was as though I couldn't stop, couldn't live just one life, couldn't be just myself. Do you see?"

"Yes, I do, a bit. But today I'm sad because I'm still not resigned to the absence of cigarettes, pens, pencils, sheets of paper. You see, you say that we still have conversation left with which to express ourselves. But we're missing the physical part of life. The fascination of gestures, colours, movements. It's true that no longer having either body or blood, your feelings and drives diminish, but without love, without falling in love, without women … More than anything else, I miss women, their softness, their shape, their warmth.

Here we're neither hot nor cold. I was about to ask myself, 'What kind of life is this?', but then you have to be resigned to not having a life any more, to this tranquillity. Living was better. This was something I was aware of even as a child, during the war. I saw that life was extraordinary and that the Germans mustn't kill either me or my sister. Then my sister chose a more serious, a more difficult path. She felt the need to vindicate herself for what they had done to us, and to acquire respectability. I didn't give that a second thought. I was always drawing and having fun. My father was an angel and encouraged me to become an artist. My life was how I wanted it, but now I'm dead I should like to tell everybody to take advantage of life, because what comes afterwards is very boring. Sorry, you don't bore me at all, but I preferred living, being in the open air, walking. Now I'm here, I don't know what will happen to me, nor even whether something *will* happen. I'm waiting, that's it, just waiting."

"I'm not at all offended. Quite the contrary! Do you think I don't understand? I miss my trips such a lot. I should like to travel, go to California again, New York, London, Argentina, Hong Kong. Now we must stay here, without ever moving! Don't tell me about it. And I don't even know how to pass the time. I don't even know if and when we shall be reborn. I know absolutely nothing about the reincarnation process and how it's decided. I can't say I'm impatient, but I do admit I'm curious to know who I shall become, what I shall become in my next life. It might be interesting to get in contact with other dead people near us here, unless they've already been reborn in other bodies."

"Hmmm. I'm still tired, I've no wish to start another life. For me, the only possible existence is the artist's. I've never wanted anything else. It would be terrible to become a bureaucrat, or a doctor, or a murderer who ends up in prison. Between being in prison and being dead, I absolutely prefer being dead! At least here we don't suffer, we have no emotions, no worries. Only if I were sure of being born as a really first class artist who could project himself into the new millennium, would I want to begin again."

"But don't you miss your family? Your girlfriends?"

"No, it's not like that. By now all contact has ceased. They own my works, and they'll do what they wish. You see, what counts are not the works that you've already produced, but the ones you have in mind, the ones that still have to be created. Do you see?"

"We don't like happiness, tranquillity makes us afraid, because it reminds us of death. Then death comes, and we feel better, because we're free of burdens, duties, suffering. What we don't know is whether we shall always be here talking together, or whether we shan't even manage to go on talking because we shall be overcome by a light sleep, a languorous drowsiness. My parents no longer talk to me, they've forgotten their French, they no longer know who I am, they talk together, whispering. Every now and again I hear murmurs, snippets of conversation. I don't even know if they are the ones who are talking. Fortunately, even after my death, I still have a visual memory of places, the memory of stories, books read, but I'm no longer afraid, either of being punished, or of losing, or of falling ill, or of confrontations with others. I'm not afraid of getting old, of being alone, of not being loved. Now I see images of my past life and these images allow me to travel in my imagination, create other images."

"So you're becoming an artist, a creator, who knows how to transform and recompose. No, that's not how I think. I don't think, don't know, don't believe. I want to hide, I want silence, I want to say 'I'm no longer here', 'I'm no longer anyone'. I don't want to remember when my sister Hélène and I were children and had to hide because the Nazis wanted to kill us. If they had killed us, I wouldn't have lived out my destiny, I would have left no trace of my life, but who cares. The Nazis, the Germans were monstrous criminals. Yes, they were, they were men gone mad, poisoned, who wanted to kill millions of innocent people. What would I feel if there were a Nazi in your place? Hate? Scorn? Yes, but curiosity as well. The desire to know how it was possible for them to work, believe in, and do their best to bring about what they called the 'final solution'. I know perfectly well that I shall be remembered as a man with an uncouth laugh. What else could I do after Auschwitz? Could I give them the satisfaction of being sad? No, we have to laugh in the faces of those human pigs who wore uniform and those who didn't and stayed silent like us dead people. Except that those who didn't speak up were afraid, whereas—as you said a short while ago—we are no longer afraid. We still know nothing, understand nothing of our destiny."

"If I had had a Nazi in the grave next to me, I wouldn't have spoken to him. I wouldn't have been curious to know why. I have removed the war, its horrors, the concentration camps. I have created a blank. But as we said, now we're dead and everything has another meaning. Since I've been here, I've not been lonely, I feel neither ill nor well. In other words, I am resigned to the fact of not being, of no longer existing, of not being a man, and of no longer having even any affection for the man I was, whereas while I was alive, I was very selfish and very jealous of my image, my character. This is probably why I had to suffer a terrible illness that disfigured me, took away all grace, all beauty, reducing me to a human larva. So you're right, in himself man is nothing, he can't understand more than so much … Of course, there are some great men, great spirits, geniuses. We already said on another occasion that we weren't at their level … "

"I've already told you, I don't want to think and I still long for some of the pleasures of life. Even though I'm dead, I seem to recall certain scents, certain moments. You see, one very positive aspect of death is that you have time to put things in order, reflect, review. Life forces us to fight, procure the means to survive. We are seized by the need to assert ourselves, to conquer, to protect ourselves. These things have vanished, pleasures are something else. Of course, I liked conquering a woman, a new love, falling in love. Those moments of uncertainty, when the affair exists, but not quite yet, when practical, material things have yet to be defined. The instant in which everything is effortless, fascinating, in which we talk about ourselves, each one telling the other his or her story. We reveal ourselves shyly, confessing to or concealing certain weaknesses. What I miss is the poetic side of life, being conquered by another person, someone you didn't know before, who suddenly, merely with a glance, becomes an intimate, becomes everything. I don't know whether you understand what I'm saying, I'm talking about falling in love, but you may consider this vulgar, unnecessary, unmanly."

"No, not at all. I too have fallen madly in love and lost my head. Of course, for me work has always been more important. Rather than seducing a woman, having an affair, placing myself in difficult and sometimes dangerous situations, I used to like the feeling that there was something between me and a woman, a mutual attraction, seduction, in short knowing that we could have an affair, but without letting it happen. You are talking about the fascination of what I call "the becoming". Being dead, things are different because our heart doesn't beat any more, we no longer have a heart, just words and memories. There's no more desire to do things. I, for example, loved riches, money, and yet that's not the way it went, no, it didn't go like that at all. Here we are, naked, just bone now, inside our coffins."

"You know, talking with you makes me think how I liked drawing, smoking, expressing my ideas. Spending the nights in bars with friends, relishing good wines. Feeling words transforming themselves into ideas, drawings, pictures ... Or else being overcome by the frenzy of writing, expressing myself."

"I liked the stock exchange. Buying, selling, earning, that I liked. Finding new stocks, new markets, new companies to invest in ... Reading financial journals, statistics, talking with stock-brokers, financial analysts. Waiting for Wall Street to open and close. Well, you'll have to excuse me, but I'm rather tired. I need to be alone, quiet."

"I'm feeling on edge. I should like to get out of this coffin and go for a walk, even just across the cemetery. Today, I'd go to see Brâncuşi. I don't speak Romanian, but I believe he spoke French. Yes, I'd really like to stay for a bit with Brâncuşi today."

While Roland and my father were talking together, alternating conversation with silence, outside Montparnasse cemetery life was going on with its ups and downs, its noises, smells, and fears. Hélène d'Almeida-Topor and Nicolas Topor went on with their lives and I, although I lived somewhere else, stayed in contact with them. In some way, the Topors and I became friends. I'm aware that Hélène has had second thoughts about what she told me during our first meeting. In actual fact, she disapproved of the fact that I had taken the liberty of investigating her brother's life and had written an imaginary dialogue between Roland and my father. She once said to me on the phone:

"Roland would not have appreciated your putting into his mouth words that he would never have used".

But Hélène must understand that my Roland is very different from hers. Her Roland is the brother with whom she spent her childhood, the one with whom she shared the same parents. My Roland has become a character, a friend, someone who has made it possible for me to make my father live again, make him talk, make him repeat yet again the stories I heard him tell so often. I should be curious to know the real Roland Topor, his anecdotes, his thoughts, but nobody wanted to reveal his secrets and everyone told me:

"If you want to know who Roland was, read his books, look at his pictures". The sole unanimous memory of Roland was his vulgar laugh, which could be heard from afar, and announced his arrival in a rather theatrical manner. I wish to thank Roland Topor, however, for his presence in Montparnasse cemetery, which will—I am sure—bring a touch of cheerfulness to my father's death. I know that Roland likes talking with someone who is so different from him, but in certain ways so like him. Although one can't be sure that the dead communicate with each other using words like the living, something certainly remains, and I think that my father and Roland feel less lonely, are better able to face bad weather, melancholy, or dark thoughts. If my father were to suffer some torment, or have a nightmare, Roland would be there ready to comfort him. Even if one of them was a night owl and the other got up early in the morning, this no longer has any meaning for the dead because day and night no longer exist. I know full well that none of us, not a single one of us, knows what happens after death, which is why we all want to know. This is the reason why Job wrote: "When man thinks, God laughs".

Venice, 14th February 1999